T0316226

Bello:

hidden talent rediscovered!

Bello is a digital only imprint of Pan Macmillan,
established to breathe new life into previously published,
classic books.

At Bello we believe in the timeless power of the imagination,
of good story, narrative and entertainment and we want to use
digital technology to ensure that many more readers
can enjoy these books into the future.

We publish in ebook and Print on Demand formats
to bring these wonderful books to new audiences.

About Bello:

www.panmacmillan.com/imprints/bello

About the author:

www.panmacmillan.com/author/andrewgarve

Andrew Garve

Andrew Garve was the pen name of Paul Winterton (1908–2001). He was born in Leicester and educated at the Hulme Grammar School, Manchester and Purley County School, Surrey, after which he took a degree in Economics at London University. He was on the staff of *The Economist* for four years, and then worked for fourteen years for the *London News Chronicle* as reporter, leader writer and foreign correspondent. He was assigned to Moscow from 1942/5, where he was also the correspondent of the BBC's Overseas Service.

After the war he turned to full-time writing of detective and adventure novels and produced more than forty-five books. His work was serialized, televised, broadcast, filmed and translated into some twenty languages. He was noted for his varied and unusual backgrounds – including Russia, newspaper offices, the West Indies, ocean sailing, the Australian outback, politics, mountaineering and forestry – and for never repeating a plot.

Andrew Garve was a founding member and first joint secretary of the Crime Writers' Association.

Andrew Garve

THE HOUSE
OF SOLDIERS

B E L L

First published in 1962 by Collins

This edition published 2012 by Bello
an imprint of Pan Macmillan, a division of Macmillan Publishers Limited
Pan Macmillan, 20 New Wharf Road, London N1 9RR
Basingstoke and Oxford
Associated companies throughout the world

www.panmacmillan.com/imprints/bello
www.curtisbrown.co.uk

ISBN 978-1-4472-1481-6 EPUB
ISBN 978-1-4472-1480-9 POD

Copyright © Andrew Garve, 1962

The right of Andrew Garve to be identified as the
author of this work has been asserted in accordance
with the Copyright, Designs and Patents Act 1988.

Visit **www.panmacmillan.com** to read more about all our books
and to buy them. You will also find features, author interviews and
news of any author events, and you can sign up for e-newsletters
so that you're always first to hear about our new releases.

Chapter One

At the Hill of Tara on that Saturday afternoon in June there was no hint of the terrifying summer ahead. James Maguire, tucked away with his books and his pipe in the snug upper room he used as a study, had been working steadily since lunch. He was a burly man of thirty-five with a broad, suntanned face and creases of good humour round. his eyes. He looked rather like a successful farmer but in fact he was a professor of archaeology at Unity College, Dublin. He had an easy-going, contented air, and with good reason, for his life so far had been singularly free from strain. His health was excellent and his work absorbed him. His salary was modest, but sufficient for his needs. He was troubled by no consuming personal ambitions. In the academic world, where the good opinion of his fellows mattered to him most, he enjoyed great respect. He had a wife to whom he was devoted, and two lively young sons. His home, a low-eaved farm-house on the western slope of Tara Hill, was remote from the hurly-burly of the city, yet accessible enough for Nora not to feel cut off from her friends—an ideal compromise. In all respects, in fact, he was a very fortunate man—and he knew it.

He was gazing out of the window, puffing reflectively at his big briar and thinking as he so often did what a pleasantly pastoral scene it was, when the telephone rang in the hall. He waited a moment to see if Nora was in the house—then went unhurriedly downstairs to answer it.

"Maguire here," he said.

A voice he didn't know, a confident, educated voice, said "Good afternoon, Mr. Maguire. My name is Sean Connor and I'm speaking for the *Dublin Record*."

"Oh, yes?"

"It's about those remarks you made at the Academy yesterday on the need for more excavation at Tara. My editor, Mr. Liam Driscoll, was very struck by what you said and entirely agrees with you."

"I'm pleased to hear that," Maguire said.

"He would like to do something about it—give the place a bit of a write-up in the *Record* and try to stir up some interest. Now if I came out this afternoon, could I have a talk with you?"

"It would be a pleasure," Maguire said. "Come any time you like—I'll be here all day ... You know the way?"

"It's off the Navan road, isn't it?"

"It is. You drive out for about twenty miles and the Hill is on your left. You'll see a small signpost if you look hard. The house stands by itself and it's the only one around here, so you can't miss it."

"Fine," Connor said. "I'll be leaving at once, then."

Maguire had had little previous contact with newspapermen and he found himself contemplating the interview with rather mixed feelings. A good article about Tara in a paper as widely read as the *Record* might be very helpful, but he remembered hearing some derogatory remarks by a colleague about the quality of local reporters when it came to writing on specialised subjects. However, his first impression of the man who drove up to the house an hour later was distinctly favourable. He was a tall, handsome fellow of thirty or so with a look of alertness and intelligence about him. He strode quickly from the car and shook hands, his assurance touched with respect.

"It's good of you to spare me the time, Mr. Maguire."

"You're very welcome," Maguire said.

The reporter eyed the house appreciatively. "What a charming place you have!"

"I find it very agreeable. It's quiet—and at the same time it has stimulating associations. I was lucky to get it."

Connor's gaze switched to the flat plain that stretched away on the west unobstructed to the horizon. "I'd no idea there'd be such a splendid view from here. There's not a hint of it from the road."

"No," Maguire said. "It's an imperceptible climb, and then the ground falls away steeply . . . Actually, the word 'Tara' means 'a place with a view,' you know."

Connor looked interested and took out a note-book.

"The Hill's five hundred feet above sea level—which is no doubt why it was chosen as an ancient stronghold. . . . You've not been here before, then?"

"I'm ashamed to say I haven't."

"Well, you share the disgrace with a great many other Dubliners," Maguire remarked with a smile. "Tara's supposed to be dear to the hearts of all Irishmen—that's why Daniel O'Connell chose the Hill for the greatest meeting of his life—but if you stopped passers-by in O'Connell Street to-day and asked them what they knew about it, I doubt if one in a hundred could tell you a thing. . . . I had an American here a fortnight ago whose taxidriver had driven him half round County Meath looking for the place."

"I can believe it," Connor said. "At least," he added, "I know a little more about it than I did yesterday. I've been reading the subject up."

"That's always a good start. . . . Well, now, what would you like to do—have a talk here, or walk round and look at the site?"

"I'd like to walk round and see the place, if that suits you."

"Very well—we can talk as we go." Maguire turned and led the way up the sloping bank behind the house.

Near the top of the hill he spotted Nora and the children in a grassy hollow. The boys were busily digging a hole with small trowels—cherished possessions which Maguire had given them and which they carried around with them as other boys might carry pocket-knives. Nora was curled up with a book in the shade of a red parasol. She had to work hard in the house, since there wasn't the money to spare for much help, but she knew how to relax.

Maguire said, "Come and meet my wife," and took Connor over. It always gave him pleasure to introduce Nora to people, for he was proud of her. She had the traditional Irish good looks—hazel eyes, long black lashes, dimples and a dazzling smile. She wasn't particularly clever, certainly not in the academic sense, but she was original and lively and affectionate, which Maguire much preferred. After eleven years of marriage, there was still no one in the world he would sooner be with.

She sat up at the sound of their voices, putting her book aside. Maguire said, "This is Sean Connor of the *Record*, darling—I'm showing him over the Hill. He's going to try and stir the public up a bit over Tara."

"Well, that's a good thing," she said, giving Connor her brilliant smile. "It's time someone did." She had never met a reporter before and she looked at him with interest. She thought him rather impressive, with his great height and powerful shoulders, his thick black hair and moustache, his easy, assured manner. His clothes fitted him well, too—unlike James's baggy old things. A man, it was evident, who took trouble over his appearance.

Maguire completed the introductions. "This is Gavin—he's nine. And that other urchin is Rory—he's seven."

The boys looked up and said "Hallo." Gavin was broad and sturdy and rather deliberate in his movements, like Maguire. Rory was more delicate in build and feature, with a mischievous, elfin touch about him. They shuffled for a moment, and then concentrated on their hole again.

"Following in Father's footsteps, are they?" Connor said.

Nora nodded. "They're like two little moles around the place."

Maguire said, "Any luck to-day, Gavin?"

"Not bad," Gavin told him. He produced from his pocket an incredibly grubby note-book with a short list of the afternoon's finds.

" 'A yelow stone'," Maguire read. " 'A snale shell. A piece of glass'. . . . Why, that's quite a haul."

Rory said, "Daddy, will I be feet first when I get to Australia? Mummy says I will."

"I wouldn't be a bit surprised." Maguire started to move on up the hill with Connor. "See you later, darling."

"How long will you be?" Nora asked.

"Oh—about an hour."

"I'll have some tea ready for you," she said.

They climbed to a tall, hideously ugly statue that dominated the skyline. "Supposed to be St. Patrick!" Maguire said, with a grimace. "An offence to Tara. . . ." He turned his back on it. "I've brought you here first so that you can get a general impression of the site."

Connor gazed around. Smooth, slightly undulating grassland, nibbled short by sheep, stretched away on all sides. Except for one or two low mounds and ditches marked with enamel plaques, and an occasional clump of bushes, it was entirely featureless. To the north there was a tiny church with a graveyard beside it; scattered over the plain there were a few isolated farmsteads. That seemed to be all.

"It's not what you'd call spectacular, is it?" Connor said. "I imagined there'd be more to see."

"The layman usually finds it disappointing at first sight," Maguire said. "The mounds were once much higher, of course, and the ditches deeper, but they've been trodden down by generations of cattle. Not many people can get excited about what they can't see, and the plaques are a poor substitute for the real thing. . . . All the same, there's not much doubt we're standing on a site that was the stronghold of the High Kings of Ireland nearly two thousand years ago. Conn of the Hundred Battles, Art the Lonely, Cormac, Niall, Leary—names we all know. Especially Cormac. He's supposed to have reigned here from 227 to 266 and to have rebuilt the place—a great many of the associations are with him. I expect you know some of the legends."

"I do now that I've read them up," Connor said, with a grin. "I even know where they were recorded—some early manuscripts, wasn't it?"

"That's right—mainly in the Book of Leinster and the Yellow Book of Lecan. They contain a sort of topographical tract in prose and verse called the Dinnsenchas—a very rich source that we're most fortunate to have. The trouble is, of course, that the very earliest text we know of doesn't date back beyond the 10th century, and if Tara was abandoned in the 6th century, as is generally supposed, there must have been a gap of four hundred years before the authors got to work. Even though some material was probably passed on by word of mouth, that's still a big gap to bridge. So the accounts in the Dinnsenchas have to be taken as a mixture of truth and fable—with fable no doubt predominating."

"But you find them interesting, all the same?" Connor said.

"Oh, very much so—fable is fine as long as it's not confused with fact. . . ! Well, now, let's get down to details. . . ." Maguire started to point out some of the monuments. "The plaques follow the Dinnsenchas," he explained. "This big oval enclosure where we are now is supposed to be the site of the Rath na Riogh, the Royal Enclosure. The two large earthworks you can see are the Royal Seat and Cormac's House. . . . That granite stone, by the way, marks the grave of Irishmen killed in the 1798 rising—there was quite a battle here. The place is also supposed to be the site of Lea Fail, the inauguration stone that roared under the feet of the rightful king. I imagine it must often have been silent. . . ! Some people claim that the pillar stone over there is the actual stone."

"If it is," Connor said drily, "the kings must have been acrobats."

"Well, there you are. . . ." They moved on to another plaque. "This mound is called the Grave Mound of the Hostages. It's ascribed to Cormac—the hostages are supposed to have been his—though the actual date is probably much earlier. . . ." They continued across the grass to more earthworks. "The Sloping Trenches," Maguire said. "I expect you've read the legend. The young Cormac is supposed to have corrected the false judgments of the reigning king here, and as a result half the house where the false judgments were given slipped down the hill. . . . In fact it's probably a burial mound, but the earthworks are certainly very unusual. It's a place that could richly repay excavation. . . ."

As they moved on again, Connor pointed ahead to a long grassy depression that ran between low banks for a distance of several hundred yards. "I've seen a picture of that somewhere," he said. "Isn't it supposed to be the site of the Banqueting Hall?"

"It is The Teach Miodhchuarta—actually the Mead Hall. It was built by Cormac, we're told, to increase the prestige of Tara throughout the country and it was reckoned to be one of the wonders of the age. In the Dinnsenchas it's also known as 'The House of a Thousand Soldiers.' "

Connor seemed to savour the name. After a moment be said, "Do you think this really *is* the site?"

"It's undoubtedly the place described by the medieval writers—there's no other that fits. And there's no practical reason why they shouldn't have been right—though, again, only excavation can give the final answer."

"The book I read called it the most intriguing spot at Tara."

"I'd agree with that," Maguire said. "All the more so because we've been left with an exceptionally full account of how the place was used. We're told that every three years or so a great Assembly was held here—the Feis of Tara. It was partly a Council of State, where laws were recited and disputes settled, and partly a great fair and an opportunity for games and general merrymaking. The proceedings seem to have started with a banquet in the Hall, presided over by the High King and attended by everyone of consequence—'the choice part of the men of Ireland,' according to the Dinnsenchas."

Connor made a note in his book. His earlier air of disappointment had now given way to a steadily growing interest. "The building would have been of wood, I suppose?"

"Of wood and thatch, with a good deal of carving and decoration. We're told it was seven hundred feet long, with seven doors on each side, and that it ran from north to south—which is how this site runs. There are actually ground plans of the building in the Book of Leinster and the Book of Lecan, though they don't entirely agree. There were supposed to be five aisles, and the outer ones were divided into compartments for the various degrees of rank, with the names of the joints of meat that each rank was entitled to. It would have been a very mixed assembly—poets, druids, merchants, charioteers, chess players, physicians, jesters, shield-makers—every kind of profession and craft. . . . In the centre aisle there were great fires, and spits for roasting boars whole, and big hanging lamps, and a huge vat for the ale. The king sat in the middle of the outer aisle, with a silver gong to strike when he wanted to command silence, and all his chiefs and champion warriors around him."

Connor was gazing at the spot as though he could almost conjure up the scene. "What a story it would have been to cover. . . !" He was silent for a moment. Then he said, "What sort of clothes would they have worn in those days?"

"At a banquet like that? Well, short tunics, anyway, and probably long flowing cloaks over them. There's a vivid description in the Dinnsenchas of King Cormac at the Assembly, with a crimson cloak fastened at his breast by a gold brooch, and a gold torque round his neck, and a girdle of gold set with precious stones. . . . His warriors would have been dressed in much the same way."

"The place must have been quite a sight."

"Indeed it must. A splendid, barbaric sight—the fires and the jewels, the harps and pipes, the gluttonous feasting and drinking, the brawling . . . But, as I say, there was more to the Assembly than just a banquet. All round the Hill there'd have been a great throng of people trading goods, buying and selling women slaves, watching horse-racing and wrestling bouts, having their fortunes told. . . ." Maguire smiled. "However, maybe we'd better leave the legends now and turn to the hard facts."

He led the way to another site, named on a plaque "Rath of the Synods," where there were signs of excavation, not very recent. "This," Maguire said, "is one of the two places where a certain amount of digging has been done—the rest of Tara is still untouched. . . . You may have read how at the end of last century two misguided individuals calling themselves British Israelites got the idea the Ark of the Covenant might be buried here and started to look for it. In those days, of course, there was no national control over digging on private land. They did an enormous amount of damage—in fact they left the place in such a mess that we felt it was a kind of challenge, so this is where we started our own digging, in 1952. . . . I say 'we,' though I was only a very junior assistant at the time so I can't take any of the credit. . . . Anyhow, we were able to date the site and trace a good deal of its history. We found post holes and trenches that had held wooden uprights and wooden palisades. We established that in the centre there had been houses of wood which had been rebuilt many times. We discovered that the people who lived here had been in touch with the Roman world—as you know, Ireland was never occupied and settled by the Romans, an important fact archeologically because it means the site was never overlaid. We found a Roman seal, a Roman lock, and some glass fragments and pottery we were able to date. We established that the history of the site extended from the 1st to the 3rd century A.D. We couldn't find any hint of extremely early beginnings, or of the Christian synods that gave the mound its legendary name, but we did find special features suggesting a ritual purpose. So you see this one small site, the least promising of all at Tara, yielded in a couple of seasons an immense amount of information."

"Fascinating!" Connor said,

"Then a year or two later," Maguire went on, "we had two more seasons over there at the Mound of the Hostages. We found about forty Bronze Age burials, a splendid series of vessels, a magnificent stone battle-axe and bronze dagger—and many other things. Each excavation, you see, throws fresh light on the period—there's hardly a limit to what we might piece together about ancient Tara if we could afford a continuous programme of digging and complete the exploration of the whole site. There'd certainly be support for some of the legendary descriptions. You may have read that a couple of superb gold torques of a spiral pattern were found here about 1810—perhaps from the neck of Cormac himself! The fact is that Tara is one of the most interesting sites in Europe, and it's terribly frustrating that work should have been stopped."

"It must be," Connor said. "I'd no idea there was so much to be discovered. . . . Is it solely a question of money?"

"It's lack of money that prevents us from carrying out a comprehensive programme," Maguire said, "and that's what is needed. If we had the funds we could employ all the trained people we required, and all the labour. But it would cost a great deal.

Excavation isn't like digging an allotment—it's a very slow, meticulous business. . . ."

"Real detective work."

"Very much the same sort of thing—and with the same care over every clue. . . . Anyhow, you probably understand now why I spoke out rather strongly at the Academy yesterday. There's a wonderful chapter of Irish history buried in this site, and at the moment it looks very much as though it's going to stay buried."

"Couldn't the money be raised?" Connor asked.

"Well, we're always trying, but there's a lot of competition for available funds. There've been some generous gifts in the past, from the Government and the universities and various outside bodies—but the well seems to have dried up."

"Surely," Connor said, "it's just a question of capturing the imagination of ordinary people—as I must say you've completely captured mine. Then they might be prepared to pay."

"Maybe—but how do you begin? When they come here they're disappointed—as you were to start with. They say there's nothing to see but a hummocky field—and one can't expect them to listen to long lectures that aren't even illustrated."

For a moment or two Connor stood gazing thoughtfully out over the Banqueting Hall site. Then he said, "You know, Mr. Maguire, there *could* be plenty for them to see. Why shouldn't that fine scene you described to me just now be reconstructed? The great House of Soldiers, the king and the champions, the feast, the fair, the horse-racing and the music? 'The harp that once through Tara's halls'—playing again. . . ! Wouldn't a scene like that bring the crowds flocking here on a fine summer day, ready to pay for their pleasure? And not just our own people—tourists, too. Think how the Americans would love it. 'The Pageant of Tara,' with all its romance and colour and splendour—why, they'd come over in thousands."

Maguire smiled. "It's an attractive thought, Mr. Connor—but I doubt if it's practicable. It would take a fantastic amount of organising."

"And what's wrong with that, if the object's worth while?"

"We should need money to start it—money we haven't got. We'd have to build the Hall, pay for costumes. . . ."

"But you'd get it back—and someone might lend you the money. . . . For that matter, I'm not sure the *Record* might not be interested—it wouldn't be the first time a newspaper had backed a fine, patriotic scheme with a bit of cash, and as I told you Mr. Driscoll is dead keen to see the excavating started again. . . . Look, would you have any objection if I mentioned it to him?"

"I'd have no objection at all," Maguire said. "But I must say I think it's too ambitious. I'll be well content if I get a stimulating article from you."

"You can definitely count on that," Connor said.

Nora was just emerging with a laden tea-tray as they reached the house. "I hope you don't mind having it out of doors, Mr. Connor," she said. "It seemed too nice a day to stay in."

"I agree. . . . It's very kind of you. . . ."

"Did you enjoy your walk round?"

"Tremendously—I can't remember when I had such an interesting afternoon. From now on I'm a devotee of Tara."

"I'm so glad." Nora placed the tray on the flat oak stump that they used as a table, and started to pour out. Then she stopped abruptly as her eye fell on the boys. They had almost finished their own tea and were facing each other, motionless, with fierce, frozen expressions. "Gavin, is something the matter . . . ? Gavin!"

Rory said, "Oh, Mummy, now you've spoilt it. . . . We were having a staring competition."

"Well, for heaven's sake go and have it somewhere else—you'll curdle the milk, making faces like that."

Gavin grinned. "We had one at our school," he confided to Connor. "The finals took twenty-five minutes. . . . I got into the semi-finals."

"You can take some cake with you," Nora said. "Rory, don't you want any cake?"

Rory nodded. "Just a slither," he said.

"A *sliver*," Maguire corrected him.

"That's what I said—a slither."

Maguire smiled and shrugged.

Nora gave them the cake and they went off, munching happily. "They're always thinking up something new and frightful," she said. "Last week they were practising sneering. Imagine!"

"Have you a family, Connor?" Maguire asked.

"No, I'm a bachelor," Connor said. "I've always been too much on the move to settle down."

"For the paper, I suppose?"

"Oh, long before that. I had several years in merchant ships, knocking around the world. Then I was in England for a while, doing various jobs. I finished up on a paper in Liverpool."

"Really?" Maguire said. "And what brought you back here?" It was common enough for young men to leave Ireland in search of work and fortune, but rare for them to return.

"Well, I happened to meet Liam Driscoll in Liverpool and he offered me a particularly tempting job—sort of roving reporting, with a fairly free hand to choose my own stories. He seemed to take to me, and I took to him, so I said 'Yes.' That was a couple of years ago, and I've been pretty well into every corner of Ireland since."

"You sound as though you've enjoyed it."

"Indeed I have. The *Record*'s, a fine paper, and I like newspaper work. A reporter is always at the hub of things."

"You don't find Ireland rather a small wheel?"

"I do, but I still like being here."

"So do I," Maguire said. "I can't think of anywhere else I'd sooner live."

"You're just an old stick-in-the-mud," Nora said, with a smile.

Connor drank his tea and put his cup down. "Well, I'd like to get this article written in time for Monday's paper, so if you'll excuse me now, Mrs. Maguire, I think I'd better be away."

"Of course," Nora said.

He got to his feet. "And thank you both very much for your kindness. . . . It's been a memorable day."

It wasn't until some time after he'd gone that Maguire mentioned

Connor's "Pageant of Tara" suggestion to Nora. He always told her things in the end, but never impulsively, never before he'd weighed them a little in his own mind.

"But, darling," she said at once, "that's a *wonderful* idea."

"It has a certain attraction," he admitted.

"Oh, you stuffy man ... ! You know very well there's nothing you want more than to get the digging started again, and this way you probably could. ... Besides, it would be tremendous fun. You'd love reconstructing that banqueting scene and bringing it all to life."

Maguire looked doubtful. "I don't exactly see myself as an impresario."

"Well, at least you could provide the material. And you could take one of the parts. Perhaps you could be Cormac—and the boys could be pages or something."

"Cormac," Maguire said, "was a graceful young warrior with flowing golden hair—'symmetrical and beautiful of form, without blemish or reproach'!"

"Oh ...!" Nora pretended to regard him appraisingly. His brown hair, as always, was unruly, his build was definitely more solid than romantic, his whole appearance was slightly shaggy. "I suppose they didn't have performing bears in those days?" she said.

Maguire chuckled. "In any case I doubt if there'd be time to do anything about it this summer. It would be a terrific undertaking."

"Not if you had the *Record* behind you—and there'd be plenty of people who'd be glad to help."

"The Hill would be bedlam all summer."

"What if it would—you'd appreciate the quiet all the more afterwards. I'm sure the boys would absolutely adore it, and I know I would."

"H'm ... Well, we'll see what happens. I don't suppose we'll hear anything more about it."

Maguire was wrong about that. Just after ten o'clock that evening the telephone rang again—and this time it was Liam Driscoll himself.

13

"I'm sorry to be troubling you so late, Mr. Maguire," the editor said, "but I'm just off to London by the night plane and I wanted to have a talk with you before I left. . . . Sean Connor has been telling me about that suggestion he made to you. What do you really think of it?"

"Well," Maguire said, after a short pause, "I think it would be splendid if it was at all practicable."

"That's exactly my own feeling. . . . Now look, Mr. Maguire, I can't make any definite promise until I've had a word with my directors and that won't be till I get back in three or four days' time, but I think it's most likely the *Record* would sponsor a Pageant of Tara."

"You do?"

"I do indeed. It's a grand, appealing idea and I think the Board will jump at it. . . . Now I don't want you to feel I'm chasing you over this but you'll agree it's going to be a rush if we're to fit anything in this summer. I'm wondering if you could get something down on paper for me to show the Board directly I get back—some sort of rough plan. Young Connor's bursting with ideas and he's an exceptionally able fellow, if you'd care to have his help. Would you be willing to meet him again and knock out something between you?"

"Why, yes, I'd be glad to."

"Then maybe you'd give him a ring and fix it—his number's 4051. I've got to hurry off now but I'll be getting in touch with you next week. Forgive me for being so abrupt."

"That's quite all right," Maguire said. "Goodbye. . . ."

He turned to Nora, who had been eagerly listening beside the phone. "Did you get that?"

"Every word," she said. "How do you feel about it now, darling?"

"A bit dazed. . . . I didn't know anyone in Ireland could move so fast."

"I suppose newspapers are all the same. . . . James, what fun! Do ring Connor."

With a feeling of slight unreality, Maguire dialled Connor's number. The reporter answered at once.

"I've just been talking to your editor," Maguire said. "He seems to like your notion."

"Like it! He's crazy about it."

"Well, that certainly does change things. ... I wonder if you could join me at the Shelbourne to-morrow morning for another talk? About eleven?"

"Sure, I'll be glad to."

"I think it might be a good idea if I asked Seamus O'Rourke to come along, too—he's the man who was in charge of Ancient Monuments, you know, before he retired."

"I've heard his name."

"There's no one in Ireland who knows more about the period, and he and I have worked closely together in the past. I'm sure his advice would be very useful."

"I'm sure it would," Connor said. "I'll took forward to seeing him. ... All right, Mr. Maguire—the Shelbourne Hotel at eleven."

Chapter Two

Maguire drove into Dublin next morning in his battered old Ford, stopping on the way to pick up Seamus O'Rourke who lived with his married daughter in a bungalow in the western suburbs. The former Director of Ancient Monuments had been a bit sceptical about the Pageant idea when Maguire had rung him earlier, but he had readily agreed to join in a meeting and discuss it.

Maguire had an immense veneration for O'Rourke—not only for his vigorous qualities of mind but also because in his day he had been an effective man of action, which Maguire couldn't imagine himself ever being. As a passionate Sinn Feiner, O'Rourke in his youth had conspired and fought fearlessly for Ireland's freedom. He had been wounded in the Easter Rising, and imprisoned for his part in it. He had suffered as a participant, and survived the long bitterness of the Civil War. Afterwards he had turned with relief to scholarship and the constructive work of safeguarding his country's ancient treasures for future generations.

Unlike Maguire, O'Rourke actually looked like an antiquarian. He was tall and spare and stooping, with a great inquisitive beak of a nose and bright, shrewd eyes. He seemed to Maguire to have aged in recent months—his white hair was sparser, his face more furrowed, his bony hands more arthritic. But mentally he appeared as alert as ever. He was clearly pleased to see Maguire again and the two men chatted for some minutes about personal matters before continuing their journey into the city.

The spacious lounge of the Shelbourne was already well-filled with the usual Sunday morning coffee-drinkers when they passed through the swing doors at half past eleven. Connor, evidently a phenomenon of punctuality, was there and keeping places for them. Maguire introduced him to O'Rourke, who greeted him in Irish—which was what he and Maguire had been talking—but switched to English when he found that Connor had little command of the language. A waiter was summoned, and brought coffee.

"Well, now," O'Rourke said, sitting back gratefully in his soft chair, "let's hear some more about this fantastic idea of yours, James."

"It was Connor who thought of it," Maguire said, "and it's the *Record* we'll be depending on if it goes through, so maybe he'd better talk first."

With a smile and a shrug, Connor proceeded to outline the plan he'd put up to Liam Driscoll the previous night. The Pageant, he said, would seek to reconstruct as much as possible of the ancient Tara scene, especially the feast in the Banqueting Hall. The idea would be to give it a romantic, patriotic appeal. There would be many other attractions as well, which would have to be discussed in detail. A big publicity drive would precede the Pageant, which the *Record* would lead. The prime object of the enterprise would be the raising of funds for the resumption of excavation. . . .

O'Rourke, listening closely, gave an occasional nod of approval as Connor enlarged on his theme—but of the man, rather than the matter. The reporter was lucid, practical, and obviously keen, and he made an excellent impression.

"Well, what do you think, Seamus?" Maguire asked finally. "A wild fantasy?—or could we do it? How does the idea appeal to you?"

"Oh, it appeals to me a lot," O'Rourke said. "It would be a fine, heartening thing if we could get a crowd of interested folk to the Hill of Tara. A great day for Ireland. . . . The question is, would it be a profitable day? Just how and where would we be raising the money to make it pay?"

Connor took a note-book from his pocket. "I jotted down a few headings on that before I came," he said. "Will I run through them?"

"Go ahead," Maguire said.

"Well, first of all we could appeal for donations as soon as the publicity was under way. Maybe we wouldn't raise much in Ireland but we'd probably pick up quite a bit in the States and other places once the object of the Pageant became known. . . . Then, of course, there'd be the entrance fees on the day. . . ."

"Entrance to the site?" O'Rourke asked.

"To the site first of all, and maybe to other things afterwards. We could charge, say, a shilling a head to go into the enclosure, and if we had a big crowd that wouldn't be a bad start. I'd say plenty of people would pay a shilling to see an old-time feast in a reconstructed Banqueting Hall."

"If there was a big crowd, how *would* they see it?" O'Rourke said. "There'd be no room to seat them."

"Maybe the sides of the building could be left open at the bottom," Connor suggested. "Then the people could sit up on the banks on both sides and watch from there. And those who couldn't sit could just file past."

"That would be all right," Maguire said, "if the feast was a sort of tableau, not a performance."

"It would be a lot easier to organise as a tableau," O'Rourke said. "I still don't see where the profit's to come from, though. Building the Hall could cost more than the takings."

"It would certainly be the biggest expense of the whole enterprise," Connor agreed, "but there are ways we could reduce it. It wouldn't have to be of very heavy construction if it was only meant to be temporary—and we could probably sell some of the timber again afterwards. The same thing goes for the costumes we'd need. If the Pageant was a success, they'd be just the sort of things tourists might like to buy as souvenirs."

O'Rourke grunted.

"Anyway," Connor said, "I haven't got anywhere near the end of my money-raising list yet. We could charge for the parking of cars and coaches, the way they always do on these occasions. We could sell programmes and literature about Tara. We could let out the catering concession—that could be tremendously valuable. Then Mr. Maguire mentioned horse-racing when we were discussing things at the Hill yesterday. If there was horse-racing at the ancient Tara, why shouldn't we have some, too? Maybe we could run our own tote."

O'Rourke grinned. "There's no doubt a lot of folk would come for the horses who wouldn't come for the Kings!"

"And there's the Fair itself," Connor went on, "the buying and selling Mr. Maguire spoke of. Maybe we could have some stalls for the sale of typical Irish products and charge for the use of them. We could have side-shows, too—all in period, of course. Wrestling matches, juggling, conjuring. A concert of folk music, maybe, for those who like it. A bit of a dance. . . ."

Maguire was impressed. "You certainly have been working on this, Connor, haven't you . . . ? Mind you, we'd bave to be careful not to make it too much of a jamboree. There'd be plenty of serious-minded people around with a genuine interest in antiquities. What could we offer them, apart from the Banqueting Hall?"

"Why not have a bit of an exhibition on the site?" O'Rourke suggested. Connor's practical enthusiasm was beginning to win him over, too. "We could show some of the actual Tara finds, I dare say, if proper arrangements were made for safeguarding them. For that matter, we could show other relics of the Bronze and Early Iron ages—a lot of people might be interested to take a look at some of the old swords and cauldrons and trumpets and horse trappings who'd never visit the National Museum on their own. We could show a whole range of Irish antiquities. We've plenty to choose from."

"A few Ogham stones, maybe?" Maguire said, smiling at the old man.

"And why not?"

"O'Rourke's the leading authority on them," Maguire explained to Connor.

Connor was looking puzzled. "Ogham stones . . . ? Oh, now, would they be something to do with some ancient writing?"

"They would, young fellow." O'Rourke's tone was faintly reproving. "Ogham is an ancient Irish script. And very interesting it is, too."

"What's it like?" Connor asked, unabashed. "I don't believe I've ever seen it."

"Now you've started something!" Maguire said, with a grin. He sat back and began to fill his pipe.

"Ogham is an alphabet of twenty-five letters,". O'Rourke said. "Twenty of them take the form of combinations of from one to five parallel strokes, arranged in various positions in relation to a central stem-line—above, or through, or below. The other five are a bit more complicated. . . . Here, I'll show you." O'Rourke took up Connor's pencil in his gnarled, arthritic hand and, with some difficulty, sketched out the Ogham alphabet on the back of an envelope. "There you are," he said. "Five vowels and twenty consonants."

Connor studied the envelope with interest. The alphabet went;

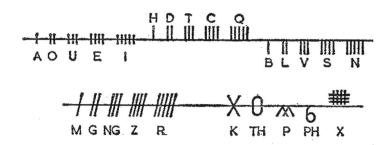

"O'Rourke is probably the only man in Ireland who has that at his fingertips," Maguire commented.

O'Rourke smiled. "It was mainly used on memorial stones," he said, "and I've worked with them so much that the alphabet's stayed in my mind."

"Fascinating!" Connor said. "Are there many of these stones?"

"We've found nearly three hundred—mostly in the south-west. The inscriptions are very brief, of course—usually no more than the name of the person commemorated, and of a relative or ancestor. The letters are scored in the stone or wood—one vertical side forms the stem-line and the letters are scored on the two adjacent faces."

Connor was still looking at the envelope. "Well, I think a few Ogham stones would make a most interesting exhibit. . . . Couldn't we even make more of it? It's just the kind of thing tourists would find intriguing. Is Ogham unique to Ireland, Mr. O'Rourke?"

"It occurs in a few other places—Wales, and Cornwall and Devon, and the Isle of Man—but it almost certainly originated in the south-west of Ireland. It's an Irish invention, all right."

"Then why shouldn't we make more of a feature of it? What about having a board at the entrance to the Pageant—some kind of welcome board, with a message to visitors explaining the purpose of the Pageant, in English and Irish and in Ogham as well. Three panels, say, in the colours of the tricolour."

"No one would be able to read the Ogham," O'Rourke said.

"But they'd be interested to see it."

"They wouldn't know what it was unless they were told."

"Well, we could have an explanatory note at the bottom of the board. It's exactly the kind of thing we need—traditional Irish things that catch the eye. ...." Connor broke off, smiling. "Or do you two gentlemen think it would be a frivolous misuse of an ancient script?"

"If it would help to raise money," Maguire said, "I'd have nothing against it. Would you, Seamus?"

"Not a thing. I'd say it was a damn good idea—I'm all for education without tears. ... There are other things we could do in the same line, too. We might try to reproduce a bit of the old village life in Ireland—some wooden huts, maybe, with an indication of the kind of activities that went on."

"We could build a cloghan," Maguire said, "a Kerry beehive hut. ... Or would that cost too much?"

"The more varied we could make the exhibits," Connor said, "the greater the attraction and the more money we'd be likely to get. ... By the way, there is one other thing, now we're back on the subject of money. As I see it, a lot of Dubliners would be interested in the Pageant who wouldn't be able to get to Tara. After all, it's twenty miles away. Now if we could have something for Dublin in the evening, something connected with the Pageant, we could take up a street collection and that might bring in quite a sum."

"It's a good point," Maguire said. "But what sort of thing?"

"Well, how about a torchlight procession—they're always popular. It would make a splendid sight—King Cormac and his chiefs parading through the streets in their fine clothes."

"They'd have to get here first," O'Rourke said with a twinkle. "What would you do—bring them from Tara in period motor-coaches?"

Connor considered. "They could come in procession all the way, for that matter, and then we could collect something in the villages along the route as well. A mounted procession. They could leave the horses outside the city if the police were afraid for the crowds, and finish the parade on foot."

"It would mean more expense," Maguire said. "There'd have to be at least a couple of hundred in the procession to make it much of a spectacle, and we'd have to hire that number of horses."

"We might be able to borrow them," Connor said. "It seems to me we're going to have to stress all along the line that we expect loans and gifts and volunteers. After all, it's a patriotic cause we'll be raising money for."

Maguire nodded. "I agree with that, of course—and in principle I think a procession is an excellent idea. It could be most spectacular. . . ."

There was a little pause. Maguire beckoned a waiter, asked the other two what they would take, and ordered two Irish whiskies and another coffee for himself.

"Well, we've covered a lot of ground," he said, "but we still haven't tackled the big question. Who would run all this? There'd be a desperate amount of organising to do."

"We'd need a strong Committee," O'Rourke said.

"Maybe you'd be chairman of the Committee, Mr. O'Rourke," Connor suggested.

The old man chuckled. "Well, now, I'd like to accommodate you, Mr. Connor, but I was seventy last week and I don't get about easily. What's more, I like to go to bed the day I get up. It wouldn't be fair to take it on."

"It's not the Committee that's worrying me," Maguire said, "*or* the chairman, but the man who's. going to do the real work. There'd obviously have to be someone in charge of the whole operation—someone behind the figureheads."

"You're the man for that, James," O'Rourke said.

Maguire shook his head. "I can organise a 'dig,' Seamus, but I couldn't handle this. Besides, I'm not a free man—I'll be tied up with lectures and seminars for some weeks yet. What we'd need is someone with drive and energy who could give his whole time to the work."

"That's true," Connor said. "We'd need a first-class man and we'd have to find him pretty soon. . . . Until we do, would you like me to act as secretary-organiser, just to get the thing started. It's not my idea—Liam Driscoll suggested it, and I'm just passing it on—but I'd be happy to act. I've an office, telephones, all the equipment, all the contacts—and it wouldn't cost the Committee anything."

"I think we should take Mr. Connor up on that," O'Rourke said promptly.

Maguire nodded. "I'm certainly for it. . . . By the way, we haven't considered yet when this Pageant would take place—assuming it did. The legendary Feast of Tara was supposed to be held on November 1st—but that's obviously too late."

"I'd say we should aim at the middle of September," O'Rourke said. "Certainly no later. The question is, could we do it in the time?"

"We'd have to," Connor said firmly. "And if we decided to, I'm sure we would."

"Well, we'll think about September," Maguire said. "Oh, there's one other thing—how far would we try to get official support for the scheme? Grants, and so on?"

"If we could get grants without strings," O'Rourke said, "I'd naturally be in favour, but if it meant a lot of bureaucratic interference I'd be against it. I've seen all I want of that."

"I'm with Mr. O'Rourke," Connor said. "I think it should be a private initiative, sponsored by the *Record*, with no interference from any outside authority. I'm sure that's how Liam Driscoll would want it. If the Pageant is held, and it's successful, it'll be because of individual enthusiasm—nothing can make up for that. Let's keep officialdom out of it."

"We'll have to get official permission to use the site, of course," O'Rourke said, "but there shouldn't be any difficulty about that. It's not as though we'd be damaging the place."

"Heaven forbid!" Maguire said. "Well, now, shall we consider who might be approached to serve on a committee . . . ?"

Chapter Three

By the time Liam Driscoll returned to Dublin, three days later, the efficient Connor had prepared a concise summary of that Sunday morning's ranging discussion, together with expressions of interest and promises of support from a number of influential people whom he and Maguire had meanwhile been sounding out by telephone. Events moved quickly after that. Driscoll, an ebullient little man of fifty, invited Maguire to dine with him and went enthusiastically over the ground. He seemed delighted by the progress that had been made and the varied suggestions that had been put forward. Next day the directors of the *Record*, at a special Board meeting, decided to open a Tara Pageant Fund with a gift of three thousand pounds, and to make a further three thousand available as a loan if it should become necessary.

With the initial expenses guaranteed there was nothing now to prevent the scheme being launched and a few days later a broadly-based committee was convened to get things going. Maguire consented to serve as chairman, and Connor was appointed temporary organiser and secretary. O'Rourke had agreed to join the Committee on condition that he would not be expected to attend more than the occasional meeting and that his advice, if desired, would be sought at his home. Liam Driscoll appeared for the *Record* at this first meeting, but said that subsequently the paper would be leaving it largely to Connor to represent it. Among the Committee were two members of the Irish Academy, an assistant director from the National Museum, a historian from Unity, a woman novelist and another woman who was associated with the Abbey Theatre, a banker, a stockbroker, a Civil Servant and a trade union leader. After Maguire had announced that official permission to use the Tara site had been granted, the Committee provisionally fixed Saturday September 15th as the date of the Pageant with the possibility of a last-minute postponement if the weather forecast should be uncompromisingly bad. Sub-committees, with the right to co-opt technical experts, were set up to deal with Publicity, Costumes, Properties, Catering, Racing, Museum, Transport, and various other matters.

At first Maguire still felt a lingering anxiety in case the project should turn out to be too ambitious after all—but as the scheme gathered momentum his doubts quickly receded. The sub-committees seemed to be settling down very well to their work and finding no difficulty in recruiting the necessary experts. Nora was certain the Pageant would be a great success and her encouragement helped him enormously. But it was Sean Connor who really gave him confidence. The more Maguire saw of Connor, the more he recognised that here was a man of quite exceptional qualities. On the first day at Tara he had seemed no more than a pleasant, intelligent reporter with some lively ideas. Now he was like someone who had realised that Opportunity had knocked for him, that this was his chance to show the world his real calibre. His stature had already grown perceptibly with his responsibilities. From being a rather quiet and deferential character, he was rapidly becoming a positive and trenchant one, with abilities that Liam Driscoll certainly hadn't exaggerated. He not only had a gift for orderly planning—he was also a dynamo of energy, generating enthusiasm in all who worked with him. By day and night he was always available for consultation, either at his office at the *Record* or at the little flat in Dublin where he lived alone. He was, Maguire found, always cool, always efficient, always to be relied on, always cheerful and optimistic. It was a rare combination of qualities, and the Committee were not long in realising what a treasure they had. The likelihood of finding a better man as secretary-organiser of the Pageant was clearly remote, and with Driscoll's consent Connor's temporary status was soon made permanent. In a short time he had become the lynch-pin of the whole scheme.

During the first few weeks the Committee watched over expenditure with a jealous, even a jaundiced, eye. The danger, as everyone knew, was that they might run through their limited resources before they had any income, and that the preparations would then come to a full stop. Connor's strongly expressed view that the greatest possible use should be made of voluntary effort, even to the point of shameless begging, was warmly approved—and in practice it worked out extraordinarily well. The construction of the Banqueting Hall, the largest single undertaking and potentially a crippling one, was successfully shared among qualified volunteers instead of being put out to expensive commercial tender. A young architect named Brogan who had done some work on an extension of the *Record* offices agreed to give his services for nothing in preparing plans for a new Hall and spent several hours with Maguire and O'Rourke at O'Rourke's house discussing the sketches in the Book of Leinster and the Book of Lecan. His final blue print was shown to several other experts, who all admired it. The architect himself found a builder, a man named Mike Donnelly, who was prepared to supervise the actual construction for no more than the value of the publicity to his business—and Donnelly provided his own foreman, a man named Regan.

An item of expenditure that could hardly be avoided was the cost of labour on the site, but here again some economy proved possible. Offers of voluntary unskilled labour had begun to come in from students and other young men whose imagination had been caught by the Tara project, and many were accepted. As for the skilled labour, applications were being received from all over Ireland in great quantity, which meant that Donnelly and his foreman were able to hand-pick their craftsmen, choosing men who could be relied on to give good value for money and who, if necessary, would be prepared to work from dawn till dusk to get the job completed. To save transport time and costs, a number of large bell-tents were borrowed from the army and erected in a loaned field under Tara Hill for the use of such of the men as were agreeable, and Donnelly himself moved into the improvised camp so that he could keep a watchful eye on things. Connor's report on these various economy measures were received by the Committee with much pleasure—but there was still better to come. The greatest achievement of all in the money-saving line was an arrangement he was able to make with a large firm of timber merchants at Dun Laoghaire by which they agreed to supply, and eventually take back, all the timber required for the various constructions on the site, at no more than the cost of deterioration and carriage.

The Costumes sub-committee were also working hard to keep costs down. The main outlay would be for the cloaks and tunics of King Cormac and—the number finally settled on—his two hundred and fifty chiefs and warriors, whose splendid appearance would be one of the principal attractions of the Banquet and the subsequent procession into town—and it was agreed that to economise there would be short-sighted. Good material would have to be bought, and skilled labour paid for. But as far as the other guests of Cormac's court were concerned, it would be a fairly simple matter to make-do-and-mend with old materials, once the period patterns had been approved, and a large voluntary sewing group was soon being organised to turn out colourful costumes for all ranks from cooks to druids. The spectacular jewellery mentioned in the Dinnsenchas—the torques and bracelets and brooches and pins—could also be made by keen amateurs, mostly from pieces of wire, with a lavish use of gold and silver paint and bits of coloured glass. At a distance, they would look real enough to get by.

The money problem remained acute for some weeks. Wages had to be paid and materials bought and transported, and in spite of all the economies the outgoings were high. Then the situation gradually eased. There was, it seemed, still magic in the name of Tara, for as the publicity got under way and the prospect of pageantry on the grand scale began to grip the popular imagination, donations started to come in. Some of them, from America, were large. On a longer view the financial outlook seemed definitely bright, for the example of the timber merchants had proved infectious and more and more firms were jumping on the band wagon of well-publicised generosity. In his mind's eye Maguire could already see his future excavating teams getting down to work at the Hill—and a very pleasant picture he found it.

It wasn't until well on in July that Maguire was sufficiently free from his academic duties to be able to give his whole time and attention to the preparations at Tara. The site was a very different place then from the tranquil hill-top he had taken Connor around a few weeks earlier. On every side there were men hard at work, single-minded as ants. Sounds of hammering and sawing and planing filled the air from morning till night. Lorries rumbled perpetually along the once-quiet lane from the main road. In the farm-house, now as much an operational headquarters as a dwelling-place, the telephone was always ringing, keeping Nora fully occupied. The appearance of the Hill itself was quite transformed. Along the shallow depression of the Teach Miodhchuarta, the vast new Banqueting Hall was beginning to take skeleton shape under the appraising eye of Mike Donnelly. Beneath its long roof, still to be thatched, the lay-out closely followed the ground plan in the Yellow Book of Lecan, with five aisles and numerous compartments, each separated from the next by a low, unobscuring wicker fence. The sides were being left open, as Connor had suggested, with the legendary doors merely indicated by thin uprights, and on the two parallel banks above, lines of smooth deal benches were being erected as reserved seats, with paths behind for walking viewers. On other parts of the Hill and its surrounding grassland, many more temporary buildings were going up—refreshment booths by the Mound of the Hostages, a Museum Hut below the Teach Cormac, the beginnings of the wooden village near the Sloping Trenches, market stalls in a field at the foot of the Hill, a "tote" pavilion, shelters, lavatories. A race-course was being marked out in the plain; car and coach parks roped off; an area set aside for folk dancing and games. Turnstiles were being placed in position near the entrance, where notices proclaimed, "No public admission until September 15th." Close by lay the sheets of five-ply for the Board of Welcome and the wooden posts which would support it. Across the road another rented field was being prepared to hold the two hundred and fifty docile hacks that would be loaned for the night of the procession—most of them, Connor had reported to a gratified Committee, already promised. Everywhere there was the hum and bustle of unremitting activity. Maguire and Nora, though troubled at times by the constant din, found the busy scene immensely stimulating. As for Gavin and Rory, they were enthralled by the goings-on. Nothing so exciting had happened in their young lives and they spent long days darting from place to place, keeping checks on the progress of each building, watching the trucks unloading timber and rushes, and speculating about the next moves. As long as they kept out of the way and merely watched, they'd been told, they had the freedom of the site—and they used it to the full.

By now the Pageant Committee was meeting several times a week in an effort to keep pace with the work. There were still a great many matters to be settled—some of them far from simple, like the problem of recruiting suitable people to take part in the banquet and procession, and arranging transport and rehearsals for them. So far no decision had been reached on that. There were a host of minor jobs, too, like drafting an appropriate message for the Board of Welcome and getting it transcribed into Ogham. In ordinary-circumstances O'Rourke, the expert, would have been the obvious man for the transcription, but he said his hands were too stiff to do all that writing and, at Connor's suggestion, Maguire agreed to do it instead.

Strolling down to the site entrance one evening, to see if any progress had been made with the Board, he found a man at work on it—an amiable-looking, red-haired young man whose name, he learned, was Boland and who came from distant Malin. Boland had joined up the posts with cross pieces and was now screwing on the first of the ply-wood panels. Maguire gave an approving nod at the neat workmanship and stood back, trying to visualise the three lots of script. It would be the task of the signwriter to fit them all in, of course, but he could see it would be quite a job to find room for the sort of text the Committee had in mind if it wasn't to be illegibly small or uncomfortably crowded.

"There'll be a few extra lines to go on the bottom panel," he said. "Do you think you could make that one a bit wider than the others?"

Boland picked out a larger piece of ply. "Sure, and why not?—there's nothing easier in the world." He demonstrated. "An extra foot, would you say?"

"That'll be about it. . . . You're making a nice job of it, Boland. Were you a carpenter in Malin?"

"Well, I was and I wasn't," Boland said cautiously. "I was a sort of odd-job man, if you know what I mean. A bit of this and a bit of that."

"Did you come down here because of the Pageant?"

"Och, no, I was in Dublin, looking for a job, and heard there might be something going here so I came along and Mr. Regan took me on."

"I see . . . There's not much work in Malin, I suppose?"

"There is not. There's work on the roads for some, and there's work in the bogs, and that's about the lot."

"And pretty poor pay?"

"Oh, you can make up to seven pounds for a six-ton lorry load of turf—but the money goes in a night."

"How's that?"

Boland grinned. "Well, now, what can a man do in that awful wilderness but drown his sorrows? He's driven to it. . . . Not that I'm after minding a dram or two of the poison myself, but it's no way to go on night after night. . . . Oh, it's a desperate place. You know what they say up there—'here's to auld Ireland and the quickest way out of it'."

"I suppose they all want to go to America?"

"They're not particular where they go, as long as they get out."

"Do you think you'll go somewhere?"

Boland gave him a curiously mischievous look. "Maybe I'll get a regular job around here," he said. He turned away, and began screwing on the second panel. Maguire watched him for a moment or two and then strolled slowly back to the house. At least, he thought, the Pageant was making some contribution to Ireland's welfare.

As the pace of construction quickened, the tented camp below the Hill had expanded rapidly. By now it was a large and well-organised colony, with its own sanitation and water supply and special cooks to prepare food and well over two hundred permanent inhabitants—carpenters and joiners, thatchers and painters and decorators, plumbers and plasterers—indeed, every variety of craftsmen, with a solid mass of unskilled labourers as well. They were mostly young, unmarried fellows, very bronzed after a month of outdoor work stripped to the waist, and remarkably earnest where the job was concerned. At night, after supper, they sometimes lit fires and sat around with bottles of stout, singing, but usually they turned in early, worn out with their labours. Maguire certainly had no complaints at all about their behaviour. Indeed, he made a point one morning of complimenting Donnelly both on their excellent discipline and on their work.

The builder, a big, muscular man of forty or so with a nose that looked as though a plank had dropped on it, gave a rather grim smile. "Well, I keep my eye on them, Mr. Maguire—but I agree they're a fine lot of fellows on the whole. It's not just the money they're working for—it's the Pageant. You can be sure of one thing—they'll never see you stuck."

Maguire nodded. "They certainly do seem keen."

"Oh, they're full of the thing—it's grand to hear them talking. ... Do you know, a couple of them asked me yesterday if there was any chance they could be in the Banqueting Hall scene, and suddenly they all wanted to be—said they'd start growing beards right away ... ! But I dare say you've got all that fixed up."

"As a matter of fact," Maguire said, "we haven't—it's coming up again at a committee meeting to-morrow and it's going to be quite a problem. ... I wonder if they'd do."

"Well, they're right here on the spot," Donnelly said, "and there's no doubt they'd take it as a mark of appreciation for the way they've kept at the job. . . . Maybe you could have a word with Mr. Connor about it?"

"I will indeed," Maguire said. "I'm glad you mentioned it."

The Committee—a very full one, with even Seamus O'Rourke managing to put in a rare attendance—gave the idea a lot of earnest thought next day. It was Connor who seemed most dubious.

"I agree they'd look fine," he said, "particularly as Cormac's chiefs—they're young and fit and sunburned and as far as appearance is concerned we couldn't do better. But could they play the parts? They're pretty simple fellows on the whole."

Mrs. O'Flaherty, from the Abbey Theatre, said, "Well, we're not going to be able to recruit two hundred and fifty actors anywhere, Mr. Connor, that's a certainty."

"If it's to be a tableau," Maguire pointed out, "there won't be a lot of playing to do. There'll be no words to learn—not much more than a little straightforward miming, I'd have thought."

O'Rourke agreed. "All they'll have to do is eat and drink and sing and swagger and laugh and ride a horse, and if those things don't come natural to every Irishman I wasn't born in Ballyshannon."

"We'll still have to recruit a lot of people for the minor parts, don't forget," Mrs. O'Flaherty said, "the druids and poets and tradesmen and so on. . . . It would be a great worry out of the way if we had the chiefs all fixed up."

"If you want my opinion," the trade union man said, "it's a good idea however you look at it. As Donnelly pointed out, those fellows are right on the spot, so they can be rehearsed at any time and there'll be no trouble fitting their clothes and we'll save pounds in transport costs. It would be a wicked shame not to use them. . . . What's more, they *have* earned the chance to take part, and they'll work all the better between now and the Pageant if they know they're going to be one of the big attractions. I'm for it."

Connor gave a faint shrug. "Well, that's all true. . . . If it's the general feeling, I'm certainly agreable."

Maguire glanced round the table. "Then we'll use the men on the spot as the chiefs, and look around for the minor characters. . ? Agreed?"

There was a chorus of assent.

"We'll have to pick the right sort of man for Cormac," O'Rourke said. "Maybe you'd like to play him, Mr. Connor? You're a fine upstanding fellow."

Connor grinned. "I'd be happy to accommodate you, Mr. O'Rourke, but I'm thinking I'll be too busy on the day to be sitting in the Banqueting Hall for hours drinking ale! Maybe I'll ride in the procession if there's a horse to spare. ... About Cormac, now—there's a man named McGrath who might do."

"A big, blond man," Maguire said, "with a wild look about him?"

"That's the fellow—he's a thatcher from Kerry. I think he'd look fine in the role. Will I see how he feels about it?"

There was another murmur of agreement.

Connor added a note to his long list of things to be done. Maguire said, not without relief, "Well, that's a bit of progress. ... Now there's the question of how we're going to recruit the other men. . . ."

As August passed, the work at the site and in Dublin became more and more hectic. Deadlines had to be watched now, and no day seemed long enough for all that had to be crammed into it. Most members of the Committee were so fully occupied with special jobs that it was difficult to meet in full session. Mrs. O'Flaherty had gone to ground in the theatres and dramatic societies and social clubs of the city, enrolling two hundred extra volunteers to take part in the banquet. Everett, one of the Academy men, was working with O'Rourke at his home in the elaboration of the old village and beehive exhibits. Moyniham, the trade unionist, was handling everything to do with tickets, refreshments, and the hiring of bands. The stockbroker was organising the "tote." Connor himself, to avoid wasting time in shuttling between Tara and the *Record* building, had transferred his office to a temporary hut near the site entrance, where three secretaries with two telephones were somehow managing to cope with the growing flood of Pageant inquiries and correspondence. So great was the pressure on him that he had taken to living under canvas with Donnelly and Regan so that he would always be on the spot if required. Maguire was no less occupied, sharing with Connor all the major decisions and responsibilities. As the tempo increased there were moments when he found himself slightly resenting a tendency in Connor to be a little overbearing, even a shade arrogant. But on the whole he couldn't have asked for a better colleague, and he certainly couldn't imagine how the Pageant would have fared without him. He said as much one evening, in a brief interval between jobs. Connor gave a short laugh. "You'll have to put up a statue to me next to St. Patrick," he said. "That'll make two eyesores ... !" His tone was light, but in an odd way Maguire felt that he wouldn't at all mind having a statue erected to him. He was a man, it was becoming clear, of considerable ambition.

As the month drew to a close, new tasks claimed attention. There were liaison meetings with the police over traffic control on the day; there were negotiations with museums over the loaning of treasures and the transport and safeguarding of them, there was the problem of receiving and storing the costumes and properties that were now pouring in. Many of them had to be stowed away in the Maguires' house, which, Nora lamented, was beginning to look like a sale-room. There were time-tables to be fixed—for the Press preview of the Pageant exhibits, for the Opening Ceremony, at which the Vice-President of the Republic had promised to officiate, for the start and finish of the Banquet, for the racing, for the procession. Masters of ceremonies and course stewards had to be appointed. Arrangements had to be made for the collection of the quiet hacks by their owners outside Dublin after Cormac and his men had finished with them. Sometimes it seemed to Maguire that order would never emerge from what at times appeared to be near-chaos, and then he would wonder aloud to Nora how he could ever have been so foolhardy as to involve himself in such a monstrously complex undertaking. But through it all Nora remained confident and Connor completely unrattled, and as the final week approached things started to sort themselves out. It began to look as though, in Mrs. O'Flaherty's words, everything might still be "all right on the night."

The weather was now one of the greatest anxieties, for after a long spell of dry heat a belt of storms had moved in from the west. In the early evening of September 8th, just after the day men had departed for Dublin, there was a deluge at the site that pinned everyone down for over an hour.

It was after the storm, as Maguire was making a tour of the buildings to satisfy himself there had been no serious damage, that he was suddenly hailed by Gavin and Rory, racing towards him from the direction of the tented camp.

He gave a quick look at their clothes as they ran up, panting. "You've managed to keep dry, then," he said.

Gavin nodded. "We sheltered in a tent . . . Daddy, we've found a box—do come and look."

"A box?" Maguire smiled. "What do you mean, found one?—there are boxes all over the place."

Rory tugged at his arm. "It was in the ground, Daddy—we dug it up."

"Oh? Where?"

"In the *tent*," Gavin said, as though his father was being extraordinarily obtuse.

Maguire frowned. "You mean to say you've been digging in a tent . . . ! Now you know you shouldn't have done that." Even as he said it, he felt that it was somehow an inadequate comment.

"We didn't mean to," Gavin said breathlessly. "We were digging where you said we could, and then it rained and there was nothing to do in the tent and we saw the ground was all bumpy where someone else had been digging so we dug too—and then we found the box."

"Well, I'd better come and have a look," Maguire said.

They climbed the Rath na Riogh and dropped down to the sodden camp. There were two men deep in conversation a couple of hundred yards away, but otherwise the place seemed deserted. The boys darted into the first bell-tent in the row, and Maguire followed them. There were eight camp-beds inside, arranged round the central post like the spokes of a wheel, with the gear of the men who lived there neatly piled on top of them. Near the side of the tent away from the opening there was a patch of ground from which the big waterproof groundsheet had been drawn back. The turf there had been cut away and Maguire could see that at some time there had been heavy digging. All that the boys had done was scoop out a shallow trench with their trowels, exposing the top of a wooden box about three feet long.

"We couldn't get it out," Rory said. "Do you think it's treasure?"

Maguire looked down at the box, his brows drawn together. After a moment he picked up a trowel and started to prise open one of the ends. A piece of wood snapped off. Inside, there was a lot of greasy paper. He snapped off more wood and pushed the paper aside ... Suddenly, he was very still.

"Is it exciting?" Rory said. "Is it treasure? Oh, do let us see."

"It's something rather important," Maguire said. "I'll tell you about it later. ... I'd like you to run along home to Mummy now—I'm going to be busy."

"Mummy isn't there," Gavin said. "She's gone to Dunshaughlin." He looked very indignant. "Can't we just look? *We* found it."

"You're to do as you're told and get along home," Maguire said, with unaccustomed sharpness.

The boys exchanged glances, got up reluctantly, and went off muttering.

Maguire quickly forced off the lid of the box and pulled out the grease-covered object. It was a brand-new sten gun. He laid it aside and heaved the box out. Underneath it there was another box, of a different shape. He broke open the corner and peered in. It was full of small, oval objects. A case of hand-grenades ... !

He was still gazing at them, in bewilderment and considerable alarm, when he heard voices at the tent entrance and two men looked in. One of them was McGrath, the blond giant from Kerry who was going to be Cormac.

Maguire said, "Go and see if you can find Mr. Connor, will you, and ask him to come here at once."

For a moment the two men stood staring open-mouthed at the gun and the boxes. Then McGrath said, "We will, sir," and they disappeared.

Maguire continued to prod around with his trowel. The dug area under the groundsheet was quite extensive. Obviously there was a pretty sizeable dump hidden there.

In a few moments he heard voices again and Connor came in, closely followed by Donnelly. Both men looked worried.

"Hallo, Maguire," Connor said. "What's all this about guns . . . ?" His eye fell on the sten, on the grenades that were now exposed. "Mother of God!" he exclaimed.

"My boys were playing around here during the storm," Maguire told him, "and they dug up a box. . . ."

Donnelly pulled back a bit more of the groundsheet and grunted. "It seems to be quite a dump. . . . I wonder how long it's been here?"

"Not long," Maguire said. "No one would pitch a tent where the ground had been cut up already—not with all the space there is around here. The stuff must have been hidden since the tent was put up."

"Then where's the loose earth?" Donnelly asked.

Connor said, "Is it packed round the outside of the tent, Mike?"

Donnelly went out to see. He was back in a moment. "No, there's nothing there."

"Then it must have been taken away and scattered," Maguire said. "I'm quite sure that this digging is new."

Connor nodded slowly. "I'd have thought so, too. . . . Who occupies this tent, Mike, do you know? We'd better have them along and see what they've got to say."

"I'd sooner leave it to the police," Maguire said. "They'll know how to handle it. . . . I'll go and call them."

"Wait now," Connor said, "we don't want to be hasty. If people get to know that an arms dump has been found here just before the Pageant they'll be afraid for their lives to come near the place. Is there any harm in keeping quiet about it till the big day's over?"

"Of course we can't do that," Maguire said. "We can't take the responsibility.—Obviously we've got to report it." He moved towards the exit.

As he moved, Connor moved too, blocking the way. Unbelievably, he had a gun in his hand.

"There are going to be no police here, Maguire," he said.

Maguire stared at him incredulously. "What on earth do you think you're doing . . . ? What *is* all this?"

"I'm afraid you've got yourself into bad trouble," Connor said, "and the fact that you did it unintentionally isn't going to help. . . . You should have taken the way out I offered you, and waited till after the Pageant."

Maguire shook his head uncomprehendingly. From where he stood he could see through the open slit of the tent. He could see men not far away. Lots of them. "You must be out of your mind, Connor. . . . I don't know what you're up to, but you seem to forget there are two hundred men out there on the site."

"You think they'll help you . . . ? Take a closer look!"

Maguire went to the opening. The construction men seemed all to have knocked off work. They were standing around in little groups, motionless, flint-eyed, watching the tent.

"You see . . . ?" Connor's smile was hard. "You haven't a friend within five miles. You provided the House of Soldiers, Maguire—I've provided the soldiers!"

His manner changed. He began to give swift orders. "Casey, guard the prisoner. . . . Shannon, mount a couple of look-outs. . . . Mike, you'd better get back to the entrance. . . ." He turned to Maguire again. "We'll be having a little talk, Maguire—later."

The tent flap fell, and the prisoner was left alone with the guard.

Chapter Four

At first Maguire found it almost impossible to adjust his mind, to accept what had happened as credible. Connor, Donnelly, all these people he had worked with so amicably for so long—suddenly with guns, and threatening him! It seemed beyond belief. The frightening world of violence was something wholly outside Maguire's experience. The only weapons he had ever had to do with were rusted treasures of antiquity. In his easy-going, sheltered life he had never encountered, nor expected to encounter, men of the kind that Connor and Donnelly had revealed themselves to be. What had just occurred in the tent seemed as wildly improbable as any fictional melodrama. Yet the sten gun and grenades were real enough; and the armed Casey, covering him from the opening; and the disciplined legion on the Hill. The facts *had* to be accepted—and the basic facts were only too plain.

Connor had been living a lie for weeks. Pretending only a dedicated interest in Tara, he had been quietly using his privileged position to build up a military camp and arsenal at the site. The Pageant had been no more to him than a cloak for his own deadly activities.

Maguire could scarely bear to think now how naively trusting he had been. Not a flicker of doubt about Connor's genuineness had ever crossed his mind. In the whole history of plotting, no one could ever have been easier to deceive and outwit than he had been. It was a humiliating thought.

How had Connor managed it? How had it all come about?

Maguire sat down on one of the camp-beds, his back deliberately turned to the guard, and lit his pipe, and forced himself with a conscious effort at calmness to go over the events of the past few weeks in the light of what he now knew. . . . Almost at once, the pieces began to fall into place.

Connor had probably intended from the beginning to use the Pageant for his own purposes. The extraordinary enthusiasm he had shown for the scheme, the vigour with which he had pressed it on Driscoll and Maguire, certainly pointed that way. So did his strong preference for keeping the arrangements unofficial. He had wanted from the start to exercise control—and obviously it had been easier for him to make himself the secretary and organiser of a committee of voluntary amateurs than of a semi-official body.

Having won that key post, he had gone on to consolidate his position. He had secured the appointment of Donnelly as the builder. Not directly—Donnelly's name had actually been put forward by the architect, Brogan—but Brogan's had been put forward by Connor. Maguire had little doubt now that Brogan was another of Connor's henchmen. So, in one way or another, the commanding heights had all been captured. No wonder everyone had been so ready to give their services for nothing!

Once Donnelly had been appointed, the rest had been comparatively easy. The choice of workers for the site had been left to Donnelly's sole discretion. Presumably a large proportion of the applicants had been already Connor's men—men he had somehow recruited earlier and who, at a word from him, had converged on Tara. Maguire could understand now why they had proved such willing workers, making up in zeal what some of them must have lacked in skill. . . . Then, at Connor's suggestion, the tented camp had been set up. Donnelly, in complete charge of the site, had filled the camp with Connor's men—and kept everyone else out. The other employees had no doubt been told that there was no more room, that they must use the daily transport provided. Needing work as they did, they would have been in no position to argue. A simple, brilliant plan. . . .

And the camp had been the perfect place to conceal arms. At least, it should have been. With ordinary luck, no one would ever have discovered anything. The arms had no doubt been brought in under cover of night, when Maguire and his family were all asleep and there was no one around. A box or two at a time, night after night. . . . Probably the whole place was stiff with weapons by now. If one tent had its secret hoard, there was no reason why the others should be empty.

So there it was—a simple reconstruction, working back from the known facts. . . . What was the purpose of it all? Some military action was clearly afoot—but what was the point of this elaborate Pageant background? Maguire could see that the Pageant gave cover for the assembly of men and the hiding of arms—but there must be more to it than that. Connor's men, after all, were to play a leading part in the actual Pageant proceedings—and by design, not by chance. It was Donnelly, Maguire remembered, who had urged that the men on the site should also be the chief actors in the drama. Connor had appeared to have doubts, but that could only have been a clever pretence, a smoke-screen. Obviously he must have approved. *Why* was it so important that Cormac's warriors should be played by Connor's men? It could hardly be anything to do with the Banquet, where they would be immobilised for hours in the full view of thousands of people.

Then it must be something to do with the procession. . . .

The procession! *Of course* . . . !

That was as far as Maguire had got when Connor returned. He entered the tent alone, after a word with the guard, and dropped down on a camp-bed near the entrance with the air of a man who had satisfactorily completed some important job.

"Well, now, Maguire," he said, "let's get things straight between us"

"What are you ?" Maguire asked. "The Irish Republican Army?"

Connor smiled. "Hardly," he said. "The I.R.A. are all right for making border forays and raiding armouries—as a matter of fact we're indebted to them for quite a lot of our weapons, among other things. But they can't tackle anything big. Their personnel is too well known to the police, their men are too closely watched. That's why something new was needed. . . ." He placed a spent match on the canvas beside him. "That's the I.R.A. . . ." Alongside the match he placed a pencil. "And that's us—the organisation that I've built up. Call it a parallel body! A much larger one, as you see."

"What are you planning?"

"To take over the country," Connor said calmly. "Nothing less."

Maguire looked at him incredulously. "You must be out of your mind. . . . You haven't a chance."

"I thought the same thing myself for some time," Connor said. "I couldn't see how it could be done. . . . The problem, of course, was to get a sufficiently large and well-trained striking force, with all its weapons, into Dublin and grouped for action, without rousing any suspicion. The recruitment wasn't too difficult. We still have plenty of patriotic young men in the country—all they needed was a first-class leader to inspire them. I filled the need. I already had quite a lot of contacts—and by taking my roving job on the *Record* I gave myself the means to develop them. . . . As you can see, I've managed to build up quite a respectable force."

He paused, as though inviting comment. Maguire said nothing.

"The training wasn't difficult either," Connor went on, after a moment. "Some of us had already had it in the British Army—and those who had were able to instruct the rest. But we were still left with the main problem unsolved—how to pass groups of heavily armed men through the streets of Dublin to their objectives without anyone realising what was happening. That was crucial if we were to achieve surprise, and I sweated on it. For a long time, I couldn't think of a solution. Then, back in June, you said your piece about Tara and the need to raise money for it. I saw possibilities there. I read the subject up, and I came to see you. What you said as you showed me round gave me the idea that finally solved my problem. The Pageant. . . ."

"And the procession."

Connor gave a sardonic smile. "I thought you wouldn't have much difficulty in working it out. . . . Exactly—the procession. You'll remember I checked with you about the clothes the warriors used to wear in the old days. The long, enveloping cloaks will give complete concealment for our arms—and we'll be in the city on

43

legitimate business. We'll be able to take up our positions after the procession without anyone suspecting a thing. Clever, don't you think?"

"Very clever," Maguire said. "But you'll still fail."

"I don't think so. The operation has been planned to the last detail. We shall strike so fast and hard that no one will know what's hit them. By the morning of the 16th every key point in Dublin will be in our hands, every political and military leader will be under lock and key. And when those who normally give orders cannot do so the people will always look for orders elsewhere."

"There are other garrisons in Ireland," Maguire said.

"They'll give little trouble, once Dublin has fallen. If they do, they'll be taken care of. This isn't going to be any desperate rising against hopeless odds. I've all the men I need—many more than are here."

"It's a pipe dream," Maguire said. "You haven't a hope—you'll be crushed."

"We shall see."

"In any case, it's a wicked enterprise. You'll cause endless suffering. What do you expect to gain by it?"

"First, the dismissal of the politicians—the spineless puppets who call themselves the Government. Afterwards, a united country—'the whole island of Ireland,' as our precious constitution puts it."

"You propose to fight the English for the northern counties?"

"Not in a pitched battle," Connor said drily. "For a start we shall be content to establish our authority south of the Border. We shall get recognition from the world for our régime. We shall drum up support in the United Nations. The English, who are already on the run everywhere, will not dare to invade us. We shall continue to press our case. Presently we shall begin to infiltrate, to erode. There are many ways of fighting for your freedom besides a frontal attack. Ask the Cypriots—ask the Algerians. Look back at our own history. We shall find ways—and in the end, the Border will go."

"You'll get no support from the people," Maguire said earnestly. There seemed little chance that he could talk Connor out of his crazy intentions, but he knew he must try. "The days for that sort of thing are over."

"You think so? 'Romantic Ireland's dead and gone, it's with O'Leary in the grave . . .'? Is that what you're saying? Three years after Yeats wrote that, the Easter Rising took place—a week of sacrificial struggle, with three thousand casualties! He was wrong then—and you're wrong now."

"Everything was different then—and the men who fought would be the first to say so. Do you think Seamus O'Rourke would join you to-day . . . ? Connor, you're living in the past. We've *got* our freedom. I don't say the Border's a dead issue, but it's not an issue to fight over, and that's the view of almost everyone in Ireland. You may have fired the imagination of a few hundred young men, but to most of this generation the Border doesn't mean a thing, and you know it. In any case, it won't be got rid of by violence—that's more likely to perpetuate it. It'll go when both sides have something to offer each other, and both sides want it to go. Most people think that's worth waiting for."

"No true patriot thinks so."

"Must a man shed his neighbour's blood to prove himself a patriot?"

"He must fight for what he believes in."

"Even when there are better ways?"

"You're a man of peace," Connor said contemptuously. "That's why you're my prisoner—that's why you don't count. The only thing the meek inherit is obscurity. Men were born to fight. What do you want to do—draw the teeth of Nature?"

"In the long run, I'd say that's the only hope for any of us."

"Well, it's the short run I'm interested in. And in the short run there's hope for the strong—the victors."

"There'll be no hope for you. It's a criminal thing you're plotting, Connor—and I'm sure you'll be frustrated."

"We must agree to differ, then, that's all," Connor said good-humouredly. "I can see I'll have to look elsewhere for the first President of the Provisional Government!"

There was a moment of silence. Then Maguire said, "You've been very frank for a conspirator."

Connor shrugged. "And why not . . . ? You already knew enough of the plan to wreck it, and you were bound to find out the rest in the course of the nest week. . . . In any case, our secret's going to be quite safe with you."

"What do you propose to do about me?"

"You're going to be silenced, Maguire. . . . Oh, don't look so alarmed, I'm not going to have you shot. I would do, without a moment's hesitation, if I thought there was no other way—but I can silence you without going to that extreme. In fact, I already have."

"What do you mean?"

"At this moment," Connor said, "your two boys are on their way to a secret hiding-place with an escort of my men."

Maguire sprang to his feet. "*No* . . . ! Connor, you can't do that."

"Take it easy, now—just sit down and listen to me." Connor waved Maguire back to the bed with his gun. "They're going to be well looked after, and as long as you and your wife co-operate with me you'll have absolutely nothing to worry about. You'll get them back safe and sound on the 16th, when we've achieved our aims. I promise that. All you have to do is to carry on with the Pageant preparations as though nothing had happened, and keep silent. . . . If, of course, so much as a whisper of our plans was breathed by either of you, the position would be entirely different. I couldn't answer then for what might happen to them."

"You wouldn't hurt them, Connor. . . . You couldn't be such a fiend."

"Look, Maguire, I don't want to harrow you, so we won't even discuss the hypothetical possibilities. But it's as well you should realise the kind of people you're dealing with. We're hard men here, and we have a stern code. A traitor or a weakling gets no mercy. Neither does anyone who stands in our way. Many of us have killed for the Cause—and many more will do so next week. There's bound to be some bloodshed. Some innocent people are bound to be shot down. It's the price of war and of victory. Some of them may be children. So you see the position. . . . The enterprise comes first."

Maguire shook his head incredulously. "I can't believe you'd deliberately harm my boys. . . ."

Connor grinned. In the pale green light of the tent he looked utterly evil, a taunting Mephistopheles. "Do you feel like taking a chance?"

Maguire was silent.

"Of course you don't," Connor said. "In your situation, no one would. So you'll keep quiet, and carry on with the work you're doing. . . . Tell me now, have you or your wife any close relatives in a distant part of Ireland . . . ? Well, speak up!"

"My wife's mother lives in Buncrana, in Donegal," Maguire said.

"Good. Then if anyone asks what has happened to the children, you will say they've been sent to stay with their grandmother in Donegal until the Pageant's over. A very sensible move, too, if I may say so—after all, they *have* caused a bit of trouble around the place, haven't they?"

Maguire groaned.

"You mustn't think I take any pleasure in this," Connor said. "I wish as much as you do that it could have been avoided. We don't see eye to eye over a number of things, but I feel no personal hostility towards you. You can't help being what you are. As for the kidnapping of children, it's a most unpleasant thing to have to do, and very inconvenient. It's melodramatic and unoriginal. But you'll agree it's effective—and what could I have done that wouldn't have been even more unpleasant?"

Maguire got slowly to his feet again. "Can I see my wife?"

"Certainly you can, if she's back. You'll find me very reasonable about everything—as long as you co-operate with me, I'll do my best to make things easy for you. My intention is that everything should go on as normally and smoothly as possible. You will continue to live at the house and move freely around. The only thing is that there will be a certain amount of surveillance. When you leave the site, as you will have to do on the business of the Pageant, you will have an escort—it may be me, it may be Donnelly, it may be someone else—who will listen to everything that's said. You will have to make it appear that you are accompanied by your own wish. All outgoing messages will be censored, and all telephone conversations listened to. I'm sure these extra precautions aren't really necessary, in view of what I've said, but I can't afford to take any risks. That's all, Maguire. . . . My last word to you is—watch yourself!"

Without speaking, Maguire turned and left the tent. As he set off over the Hill back to the house, two men followed behind him at the same pace.

Chapter Five

The Ford, he saw, was back in the garage—which meant that Nora was home. As he approached the house he caught the sound of radio laughter from the portable set in the kitchen. Obviously she knew nothing. He paused for a moment at the front door, steeling himself to the ordeal of telling her. One of the men who had been following him strolled up and silently stationed himself on the step. Maguire went on in.

Nora called, "Is that you, darling?" and came out into the hall, smiling. "You haven't seen the children, have you?—it's time they were . . ." She broke off as she saw his face. "James, what on earth's the matter?"

"There's been some trouble on the site," he said. He took her back into the kitchen and closed the door and switched off the radio. "Bad trouble—almost unbelievable. . . . Nora, Connor isn't what he seemed to be. Neither are the men. They're all in a plot to stage a rising in Dublin on the 15th. They've simply been using the Pageant as a cover. . . ." In a few sentences, he told her of the find in the tent, of the armed camp around them, of how he'd been held prisoner, of Connor's plans.

Nora stared at him, incredulous, aghast. Like Maguire, she had taken Connor completely at his face value. It seemed impossible. . . .

"Mother of God!" she breathed. "What have we got ourselves into?"

"I'm afraid that's not all. . . . Nora, this is going to be a shock for you—you must take hold of yourself. . . . Connor has had Gavin and Rory taken away as hostages to make sure we don't talk. He's going to keep them till after the 15th."

49

Nora stood as though paralysed, her whole world suddenly crumbled around her.

"But they're going to be quite all right," Maguire went on quickly. "They'll come to no harm. Connor swears they'll be well looked after and treated kindly and I'm sure they will be. These men are misguided but they're not really wicked or cruel. . . . And Connor is only holding the boys as a guarantee of our silence—he'll have no interest in them after the 15th. In a week's time we'll have them back safe and sound. . . ." Even as the facile words came tumbling out, Maguire felt that things might not be as simple as that. But for the moment he could think only of Nora.

She had slumped down on one of the kitchen chairs. She looked dazed, shattered. "Do you know where he's sent them?"

Maguire shook his head. "It could be anywhere."

"What can we *do*?"

"I can't see that we can do anything at the moment—Connor has got us in the hollow of his hand. . . . He said if we made any move he wouldn't be answerable for the boys' safety."

Fear leapt into Nora's eyes. "God . . . ! Then we can't."

"In any case," Maguire said, "we're both going to be watched all the time."

"Do you suppose he'd let us have them back if we promised to keep quiet?"

"There's not a chance, Nora—he'd never trust us. He's got too much at stake." The lines of Maguire's face tightened. "Besides, I wouldn't give him a promise. We can't tell what may happen. . . ."

They were silent for a moment, staring at each other. Then Nora said, "Were you there when they were taken away?"

"No—I was in the tent. I'd sent them back here to be out of the way—it never occurred to me that anything like this could happen. . . . But I couldn't have stopped it."

"I suppose they were just snatched up and bundled off . . . ! They must be terrified. . . ." An unbearable picture was forming in her mind. "James, they'll be so lonely, they won't know what's happened, they'll wonder why we don't come. . . ."

"It may not be as bad as that," Maguire said. "They were probably told something—some story. ... And they've got each other ... it's lucky they get on so well together."

Nora wasn't listening. "I don't suppose they've got -any of their things with them," she said. She got up suddenly and rushed out. Maguire heard her rummaging in the cloak-room, in the boys' room upstairs,, She was back in a few moments, looking more anxious than ever.

"Their clothes are all here—they've nothing but what they were wearing. Just shirts and trousers. ... Suppose they're shut up in some horrible, damp place. It's only a week or two since Rory got over his cough. ..."

"I'm sure they'll be all right," Maguire said. "The weather's warm—and if they need clothes I expect they'll be given them. ... You mustn't imagine things."

"How can I help it when I don't *know*?"

"It's only for a few days."

"It'll seem like a year. ..."

She stood looking at him, her eyes staring out of her white, drawn face. There was not only pain there, and fear—there was bitter, helpless frustration. It was not being able to do anything, Maguire knew, that was the worst thing of all for her—the feeling of utter impotence, when every instinct cried for action.

"If only I could see them," she said. "If only I could be *sure* they were all right. ..."

The anguish in her voice was almost more than Maguire could bear. Desperately, he sought to comfort her. "Maybe Connor will let you visit them ..."

The words had an immediate, a galvanic effect on her. "James—do you really think he might?"

"It's possible. ..." She had clutched so eagerly at the faint hope that he almost wished he hadn't said anything—but it was too late to draw back now. "After all, he did say he'd make things as easy for us as he could."

"But would he want me to know where they were?"

"I'm sure he wouldn't let that happen—he'd have to take precautions so that you didn't find out."

"Like covering my eyes, you mean, or waiting till it was dark?"

"Something like that."

"Then he wouldn't lose anything by it, would he ?"

"I can't see why he should."

"Oh, it would make such a difference. If I could just see for myself ... !"

"You mustn't bank on it," Maguire said. "He may turn us down flat. The place may be too far off. . . . It would be a horrible journey for you, anyway."

"I wouldn't mind what it was like as long as I could see them. I'd put up with anything. . . ."

"Well," Maguire said, "we can only try. I'll ask him about it first thing in the morning."

Chapter Six

The morning was a long way off, though—for both of them. First, there was the evening and the night to be endured. The initial shock was over, but an aching anxiety filled them and grew worse in the familiar surroundings of the house. Hardest of all, for Nora, was the silence of the boys' room—the unbearable emptiness, contrasting so sharply with the accustomed cheerful ritual of supper, bed and story. Why, they had never even been away from her before. ... She tried not to dwell on it, but it was beyond her power to discipline her mind. Her thoughts returned constantly to the children—to where they might be, whether they had proper bedding, what they'd been told, what effect their brutal seizure might ultimately have on them. Maguire tried to reassure her. Boys were resilient creatures, he said—and when eventually they were told the whole story it was as likely as not they'd see it all as an exciting game of cops and robbers and be proud of their part in it. ... Nora seemed a little consoled by that.

Maguire's own anxieties went beyond the immediate personal ones. Not for a moment could he get out of his mind the thought of Connor's lethal preparations, of the guns and grenades in the tents, of the awful carnage that might spread through Dublin once they started to go off. The burden of his secret knowledge weighed on him intolerably. He alone had the power to prevent the worst. If he spoke out, the rising would be crushed before it started. Yet how could he speak out? Already he foresaw a hideous clash of loyalties and responsibilities—to Nora, whom he loved and cherished, to the two small boys he was so proud of—and to the scores of decent, ordinary, anonymous people whose lives were also in his hands. . . . If only he could think of a way out—a *safe* way. . . .

Conversation through the long evening came in brief, disjointed bursts. Old ground was covered again and again, until there seemed nothing more to be said. Then, for a while, Nora herself stopped concentrating on her private misery and showed awareness of the larger issue. What, she asked Maguire, would Connor actually do on the 15th—and what were his chances of success? He told her, as he'd told Connor, that in his view the rising couldn't succeed—but that there would be a bloody shambles all the same. They talked for a time of Connor and his fantastic hopes. Anger suddenly flared in Nora, as the arrogance of what he was doing was borne in on her—but anger seemed futile, and it soon died, to be followed by depression again. The only productive discussion they had was about the best tactical approach to Connor in the morning.

The few essential chores around the house were a slight relief, an active alternative to sitting and thinking. Nora got supper, though neither of them felt hungry. Maguire helped her to wash up afterwards, just to be close to her. He had never needed her companionship more. Both of them ignored Connor's guard, who had now moved uninvited into the hall and was sitting at the telephone table with his gun beside him. He was a man named Murphy, a plasterer from Wicklow, whom Maguire had found quite talkative on the site. Now he sat in a heavy silence, avoiding Maguire's eye.

It was from habit, not from inclination, that they finally went up to bed. They both felt exhausted, but neither expected to sleep. Nora got into bed and lay there, open-eyed, reliving the awful hours and thinking about the children. Maguire sat for a long time by the window, looking out. He could just make out the figure of a second guard, strategically placed to watch both the front and the back door. Connor was certainly taking no chances.

Maguire found it hard to understand Connor. Some of the qualities the man had shown undoubtedly went with the sort of role he was filling now—the magnetic personality, the gift of persuasion and leadership, the dynamic energy and drive. But others didn't. He had always seemed to Maguire an extremely practical and down-to-earth figure—not at all the kind of man to commit himself to the folly of an armed revolt against a stable government elected by his own countrymen. There was, Maguire knew, a streak of irrationality in many Irishmen, a stubborn preference for the rosy view of prospects, a fatal tendency for the heart to sway the head. Maybe Connor was like that. Yet there were still contradictions. Down there in the tent he had talked like a romantic patriot, a visionary, a dreamer—yet what sort of an Irish dreamer was it who had never troubled to read the legends of Tara, who hadn't even bothered to learn his country's language? One thing seemed clear—he was a far more complex character than he'd appeared to be. A vain man, maybe, determined to leave a mark, dramatising himself in a spotlight. Putting on a play to outrival Cormac! Not caring, or perhaps not fully realising, that the make-believe must end in tragedy? It was hard to know. ... Who could tell what drove a man on?

Connor was at the house before eight next morning. He knocked and waited with derisive courtesy to be invited in, though his guard was still in possession in the hall. Maguire, unshaved and in his dressing-gown, was preparing a breakfast tray in the kitchen. After a moment he went to the door and opened it.

"Good morning to you!" Connor said. "It's on the early side, I know, but I thought maybe I should drop in and make sure everything was all right." He looked spruce and cheerful. Maguire, after an appalling night, felt like death—though in the circumstances that was probably just as well. He would certainly have to make no great effort to play convincingly the scene that he and Nora had planned".

"I hope my fellows aren't bothering you too much," Connor said. "It must seem a frightful intrusion, having strangers in and around the house all the time—but they're well-disposed to you. If there's any little thing they can do for you, they'll be glad to."

"They're no bother," Maguire said curtly. "And we don't need their help."

"As you please. . . . Well, how's your wife taken it?"

"How do you think? She's almost out of her mind with worry."

"I'm sorry to hear that," Connor said. "As I told you last night, I wish it could have been avoided."

"Have you any news of the children ?"

"Not yet—but I don't doubt they're well, and taking nourishment. I've given precise orders about the way they're to be treated—and my orders are always obeyed to the letter. . . ." He eyed the breakfast tray. "I hope you're not going to be too long over your domestic arrangements—we've a busy day ahead, There are several new things I want to put before the Committee this afternoon, and I'd like to go over them with you as soon as you're ready."

Maguire looked at him apathetically. Connor's tone grew sharper. "You'd better pull yourself together, Maguire, and start showing some interest again. It's part of the deal, you know."

"It's impossible," Maguire burst out. "Damn it, Connor, I'm flesh and blood. How do you expect me to concentrate when I'm worried to death?"

"About the children? You don't need to be. I keep telling you they're perfectly all right."

"About Nora, more than the children. She's almost beside herself, Connor. She's had a hell of a night and she's going to have a hell of a day. She can't believe they're all right. She imagines them terrified, screaming themselves sick. She's fretting all the time. And while she's like that I can't think of anything else."

Connor frowned. "Can't you give her a sedative?"

"The only sedative that'll do her any good is to see for herself that the children are well and reasonably happy. . . . For God's sake, man, try and put yourself in her place. The boys are only seven and nine and they've always been close to her. Now she doesn't even know whether they've got a roof over their heads. I tell you frankly, if things go on like this she'll be breaking down altogether—and then you won't get any sense out of me even if you stand over me with a gun. . . . Would it hurt you to let her go and see the children?"

Connor regarded him thoughtfully. "You think that would help?"

"Of course it would help—it would make all the difference. She could satisfy herself they were being properly looked after. She could tell them something to settle their minds. And she could take their things along—their clothes and toothbrushes and toys. That may not mean much to you but it would mean a lot to her."

"I can have them sent," Connor said. "In fact, I'd already planned to do so."

"It wouldn't be the same. . . . She needs to see the boys herself, to talk to them. It's the only thing that'll reassure her."

"H'm. . . ." Connor was silent for a while. Then he said, "It's quite a journey she'd have to make."

"If it was to the other side of Ireland it would be all the same to her."

"Oh, it's not as far as that. . . . It would be a late journey, though—you could hardly expect me to let her go in daylight. . . . Not that I think either of you would try any tricks, but the less you know the better."

"She'd go wherever you said. She'd do exactly as you told her."

"You've discussed it with her, have you?"

Maguire nodded. "I promised to ask you. It was the only way to stop her crying. You can't imagine what it's been like. . . ."

"It would be a very uncomfortable journey for her," Connor said. "Does she realise that?"

"She wouldn't care, Connor—don't you understand? All she wants is to see the children—she'd put up with anything to get to them . . . And if you've got any sense you'll let her go."

Connor pondered.

"Very well," he said at last. "She can go at dusk this evening and spend an hour with them. I'll see to the arrangements. You can expect her back around midnight."

Maguire picked up the tray. "I'll go and get dressed," he said.

It was a fantastically unreal day at Tara. Maguire, concerned for the moment only to safeguard the concession he'd won, behaved outwardly as though nothing had changed at the site, made his rounds as usual, and joined with Connor in taking Pageant decisions which no longer had the slightest interest for him. Nora, physically jaded after her sleepless night but enormously relieved in her mind at the prospect of seeing the children, managed to go through the motions of answering the telephone and taking messages for Maguire as she'd always done. The Hill itself looked as innocently active as ever, with groups of labourers busy on their varied jobs, Donnelly deep in technical discussions with the foreman, the office a humming hive, people arriving to see Connor, and cars and lorries constantly loading and unloading at the entrance. Not a hint of the underlying drama obtruded anywhere—and none, Maguire thought gloomily, was likely to. No one else would be given a chance to discover those buried arms. Everything would appear normal now until the planned eruption.

Even the attitude of the men to Maguire seemed not to have changed very much. Connor's order that everything should be made easy for him was obviously being carried out to the letter. There was a slight wariness, perhaps—a trace of self-consciousness at his approach—but, with rare exceptions, that was all. There was certainly no sign of general animosity. Most of the men seemed rather sorry for him. Those that Connor had assigned to guard duties were especially considerate—though they were none the less efficient for that. Not for an instant was the telephone left unattended or the house unwatched. When, during the morning, Nora said she needed some things from the village, one of the guards borrowed her bicycle and went off to do her shopping for her. Wherever Maguire went on the site, he was aware of a shadow not far away. If he happened to approach any of the day men, anyone who was not in the plot, someone would appear instantly at his side to overhear and join in the conversation. Privacy, except with Nora, was a thing of the past.

As Maguire moved around, he found himself studying the men with a new, almost clinical curiosity. It seemed beyond belief that so many should have been prepared to risk their lives and fortunes in this violent, desperate enterprise which was so out of tune with the times. What were their motives? As far as he could see, they had little in common except their youth. They were certainly not a physical or mental élite—but neither were they a band of ruffians, for all their ferociously-sprouting beards. Some were gaunt and hollow-eyed, and looked as though for years they had gone short of nourishment. Poverty, and lack of prospects, could have driven those into Connor's camp. Some had an air of lively intelligence—a questing, student air. A few were furtive, as though aware of guilt, but it could have been no more than a cast of countenance. Some had the gift of the gab, and ready smiles. Some had simple, mindless faces, the faces of men who would always do the dirty work of the world at someone else's bidding. Some were handsome and proud and soldierly, with a look of Michael Collins about them. Some had the uneasy swagger of city teddy boys—types who everywhere had to find some outlet for their dangerous energies. Some looked mere bullies, hulking natural gangsters. Some had the unmistakable glow of idealism in their eyes, the fanatical intensity of incipient martyrs. Maguire could detect no basic similarity anywhere, except in one respect—their air of disciplined purpose and loyalty to their leader. Connor, of course, was the common factor—Connor, who stood head and shoulders above them all. It was Connor's twisted genius, working on their hopes and fears and uncertainties, inflaming and inspiring when it could and no doubt bribing too with the promise of excitement and glory and reward, that had brought them all together under a common flag.

Little though he felt like it, Maguire was given no choice but to attend the meeting of the Pageant Committee that had been arranged for that afternoon in Dublin. Connor drove him in and sat beside him at the table. For Maguire the session was an unmixed ordeal. With a dozen friendly people around him, he now had his first opportunity to unmask the plot if he dared. Yet he was compelled by every circumstance to keep silent—by the gun he knew must be in Connor's pocket, by the certainty that Connor would make his escape at the first sign of trouble and be free to take revenge, by his own ignorance even of where the children were. Connor at no time showed any uneasiness about what Maguire might do. His manner was relaxed, his handling of the matters that came up as briskly competent as ever. Obviously he had a nerve of iron. He was certainly much less under strain than Maguire himself, who had to make a constant effort to focus his mind on the discussion and appear in normal spirits.

It was a relief to get back to the house in the evening—there, at least, Maguire could throw off all pretence. The guard at the telephone gave him a slightly embarrassed grin as he passed through the hall and he recognised Boland, the red-haired handyman from Donegal whom he'd rather taken to. He went on upstairs, the only private part of the house now, and found Nora in the boys' room. She asked him about the meeting and he told her how it had gone, quite briefly. She listened with a somewhat preoccupied air. She was packing a suitcase with the clothes and belongings that the children would need, and her main concern at the moment was that nothing should be overlooked. Maguire glanced over the toys, but could think of nothing to add. The boys' trowels, he saw, were already in. Presently she closed the case and he took it downstairs for her. In the hall Boland jumped up and insisted on carrying it to the door. . . . It was hard, Maguire thought, to see Boland as a potential assassin.

Now there was little to do but wait for Nora's transport. She had still been told nothing about her coming journey beyond the fact that it was to start at dusk, but she seemed quite indifferent to the arrangements. Not even the prospect of having to travel blindfold for hours seemed to worry her. Maguire, noting the marks of strain and fatigue in her face, felt more concern. He wished now that he could have gone instead of her, or at least accompanied her—but he didn't suppose Connor would take kindly to the idea at this stage, and Nora was anxious not to do anything that might upset the plan. She would be quite all right, she said—she would try to get some rest on the way.

It was just before nine when a plain, closed van drove up to the front door. From the window, Maguire saw the builder, Donnelly, get out and lift the suitcase into the back of the van. The driver was an intense, romantic fellow named Kelly who had been chosen to play a harp at the Banquet. There was no sign of Connor.

Maguire said, "They're here, darling," For a moment he held Nora in his arms. "Look after yourself," he said. "Give the boys my love and tell them I hope to see them soon."

"I will."

Maguire lowered his voice. "I don't suppose you'll be able to see much but there's just a chance you might hear something on the way. Odd sounds as you go through places—that sort of thing. You never know what might come in useful."

Nora's eyes lit up with interest, but she only said, "Yes, all right."

They went down together. Donnelly was standing by the rear doors. "Would you mind getting in here, Mrs. Maguire?" he said politely. "It's not what you'd call the height of luxury, but we've done our best to make it comfortable for you."

Maguire peered into the van. It was an old, battered vehicle. A sliding door, separating the body from the driving-compartment, was closed, and there were no windows—but there was a big revolving ventilator in the roof. There were no seats, but a pile of rugs had been spread on the floor. Maguire helped Nora to climb up. "It seems I'm not to be blind-folded after all," she said, attempting a smile. She gave a little wave, and Donnelly closed the doors and returned to the passenger seat. A moment later the van was away.

As it disappeared round the hill, its lights bright in the darkness, the outside guard said, "Will you do me the favour of going into the house now for a while, Mr. Maguire? It's the Captain's orders."

In silence, Maguire went indoors. Evidently he wasn't to be allowed to see even the initial route the van took.

At first Nora was so thrown around inside the van that all she could think of was holding on. There were several sharp corners in the road, and at every turn her body swayed violently. They were well-known corners—this was home ground. Soon, though, she lost track of them. The motion of the van grew steadier. She found a way of bracing her feet so that she could keep herself from lurching. The floor was hard, in spite of the rugs, but she was more comfortable than she'd expected to be.

In the pitch-black interior she could see nothing at all. Presently she settled down to listen. She would never have thought of doing so if Maguire hadn't suggested it, and she wasn't at all sure what he wanted her to listen to, but at least it helped to pass the time. She was an experienced driver, and though the van was unfamiliar she had no difficulty in recognising each gear change. There were other distinctive sounds, too—the whir of the ventilator in the roof, the hum of the transmission under the floor, the wheels rumbling on the road. Sometimes the rumbling note changed as they ran on to a different surface. She found she could tell when they passed a building that lay very close to the road, because the sound of their passage was reflected back. But that didn't happen often. Most of the time they seemed to be travelling through completely empty country. The van kept going at a steady, moderate speed, with no checks. The driver wasn't using his gears at all now. There was practically no other traffic. Nora knew when they passed anything with lights because for a moment or two there was a glow through the revolving ventilator. That also only happened once or twice. For the most part the journey was entirely without incident, and presently she gave up the unrewarding task of listening and began to think again about the children, and what she should say to them.

The drive seemed endless. It was too dark for her to see her watch and she could only guess at the time. Once Donnelly opened the sliding door an inch or two and asked her if she was all right and she said she was. Then darkness fell again, and she lost track of everything. . . . She was actually asleep when the van pulled up. She woke with a jerk, her heart pounding.

The doors at the back of the van opened. In the light of the tail lamp she could just make out Donnelly's bulk. "We've arrived, Mrs. Maguire," he said. "I'll have to ask you to cover your eyes, now, just while we go in." He had a silk scarf in his hand and he tied it round her head himself. Then someone took her hand, and strong arms lifted her out.

"Before you see the children," Donnelly said, "there are one or two things you'd better know. First of all, what they think has been happening. . . . They've been told that you and your husband asked that they should be brought here by one of the men, MacEoin, for a holiday, because you were both very busy. . . ." Donnelly went into some detail about the story, Nora listened carefully.

"They've accepted that," Donnelly said in conclusion, "so if you want to keep them happy you'll stick to it. . . . Then there's a word of warning I must give you. It's no use asking them where this place is, because they don't know. They think they do, but what they've been told isn't the truth. They wouldn't be able to tell you how they got here, either, because they were taken somewhere else first and only brought here after dark. Mr. Connor thought of everything, you see. . . . And don't try and get them to describe the place, or your visit will end right away. Lay off the subject altogether. The door will be open—we'll be listening and keeping an eye on you. . . . Understand?"

"I understand," Nora said.

"Then I'll take you in."

She felt herself being guided forward. Her footfalls were quiet, as though she were walking on grass. She could smell peat smoke in the air. A warm fugginess told her that she had entered a building. The hands still guided her. "Up the stairs, now," Donnelly said. "Take your time." She started to climb.

Suddenly an excited voice from above cried, "*Mummy* . . . ! Rory, wake up—it's Mummy!"

In a moment someone unfastened the scarf, and Nora saw an open door ahead, a lighted room, and rushed inside.

Chapter Seven

Back at Tara, Maguire had been allowed to leave the house again and was pacing slowly up and down in the drive under the light of an outside lamp. Nora had been gone for a little over half an hour. The guards had just been changed. A man named Kennedy had taken the place of the watcher on the hill-side, and Boland had been relieved at the telephone by a stocky youth named Everett. Boland was still in the hall, chatting to Everett.

Maguire was deep in thought, and not just about the situation in general. He was wondering about Nora's unknown destination. It had seemed a pretty hopeless subject for speculation before her departure, and his suggestion that she should listen had been made without any serious expectation of results. What had suddenly set him thinking about it again was the fact that he'd been told to go indoors as the van left. He'd found that most intriguing. "Why," he'd asked himself, should it have mattered so much that he shouldn't see the direction it had taken to start with, if—as Connor had said—the place where the children were hidden was a long way off? The knowledge that the van had set off to the north, or the west, or the south wouldn't have given him any clue to a destination, say, forty miles away—the precaution would have been quite pointless. . . . Was it possible, after all, that the place *wasn't* so far away . . . ?

It was true that Nora had left the house at nine and that she wasn't going to be back until midnight—and Connor had said she would only have an hour with the children. That seemed to mean an hour each way for the journey. But a journey could easily be made to last longer than it need. Indeed, the nearer the place, the more likely it was that the driver would have been instructed to take a roundabout route. It was the sort of thing Connor might well have thought of.

Was there any way he could find out about that?

Maguire wondered if the guards knew where the place was. He had no means of telling—they might, or they might not. . . . If they did, they obviously wouldn't give anything away. . . . At least, not consciously.

What about unconsciously? Was there a chance, perhaps, that he might get the information by some subterfuge . . . ? He frowned in thought. . . . Suppose he told them he'd suddenly remembered something that he had to communicate to Donnelly urgently—something to do with the Pageant? Suppose he said it was vital that a message should be taken right away? He might be able to tell from their manner whether they knew where the place was, and whether it was near enough for a quick trip. . . .

No, that wouldn't do. Connor would be sure to hear about it. He'd know that there couldn't have been any message for Donnelly as urgent as that. He'd know that Maguire had merely been seeking information. And Maguire didn't want Connor to know the lines on which his thoughts had begun to run. For one thing, he'd be put on his guard—and for another, he might turn very ugly.

Was there any sort of message that would seem reasonable and legitimate even to Connor? An urgent message to Nora, perhaps? Something about the children—an afterthought? Something Maguire had forgotten to tell her. . . .

He stopped short, as another idea occurred to him. What about something she'd forgotten to *take?* Something that the children would want, that had been overlooked. . . . Connor would have no reason to be suspicious about that.

The notion grew in his mind. . . . There might even be an outside chance that he could actually get something taken, if the place was near enough. Boland might agree to go—he seemed to be at a loose end. . . . New, exciting possibilities suggested themselves. . . . There was certainly nothing to be lost by trying.

Maguire stood for a moment or two, working out a plan. Then

he went indoors, past the two men in the hall, and on upstairs. From a cupboard in the boys' room, a repository of abandoned toys, he selected a decrepit old Teddy-bear. He waited for a while, so that it shouldn't seem as though he'd gone up specially to get it. Through the open door he could hear the voices of the men below. Presently he heard Boland say, "Well, I'm away now. . . ." He went out on to the landing and stood listening. The voices had stopped. He continued on down. Boland was just leaving the house. The new telephone guard looked curiously at the Teddy-bear, but said nothing. Maguire rushed out. Boland was walking slowly away along the drive. He glanced round when he heard footsteps behind him—and stopped.

"Now what in the name of God would you be doing with that, Mr. Maguire?" he asked, as Maguire came up with him, clutching the bear.

"It's Rory's," Maguire said, "the small fellow's. It's the one thing he'll ask for. My wife must have thought she'd put it in the suitcase, but there it was on the floor. . . . He'll be heart-broken."

Boland looked concerned. "Why, that's an awful thing," he said. "Are you off duty now?"

"I am."

"I suppose you couldn't go after them with it?"

Boland hesitated—and two of Maguire's unspoken questions were answered. Obviously Boland knew where the place was—and it couldn't be too far away, or he'd have said so at once.

"Can you drive?" Maguire asked.

"I can that."

"Then, you could take my car. . . . I'd be very grateful to you, Boland. The boy will be terribly upset if he doesn't get it—and it's desperate enough for him as it is, having to do without his mother and all that."

"Well, I don't know. . . ." Boland still hesitated. "I'm not sure Mr. Donnelly would like me butting in. . . . Maybe I could just leave it at the door for you. I reckon there'd be no harm in that."

"It would do fine," Maguire said eagerly. "Rory would be sure to find it in the morning. . . . And there'd be a bottle of Irish for you when you got back."

Boland grinned. "Would you be after bribing me, Mr. Maguire?"

"Not at all," Maguire said. "But a generous action's none the worse for a bit of recognition. It would be for your trouble."

"Well, if you put it like that, I'll have no objection." Boland took the bear. "Why, all the stuffing's coming out," he said. "Now why would anyone be wanting a thing like that?"

"Children always like old toys best," Maguire said. He walked with Boland to the garage, switched on the light, opened the car door, and showed him the gears.

He also read the mileage on the speedometer.

Kennedy, the hill-side guard, came strolling up. "And where would you be going, Tim?" he asked.

"I'm going to take this over for Mr. Maguire's boy," Boland said, showing the bear. "It got overlooked in all the rush, and the little fellow will be eating his heart out."

The guard gave an indifferent nod. Boland climbed into the car, reversed out of the garage with a crash of gears, found bottom gear with another crash, and roared triumphantly away down the drive.

"Better go into the house, Mr. Maguire," Kennedy said.

Maguire waited, with what patience he could muster. It looked as though his trick was going to work, but he couldn't be sure until Boland returned. The man might run into trouble with Donnelly—though Maguire couldn't see why he should, since he was only doing what Connor had said they were all to do, make things easy for himself and Nora. . . . Anyway, there shouldn't be long to wait. Maguire knew for a certainty, now, that the children weren't very far away. But even he wasn't prepared for the return of the car less than half an hour after it had left. For a moment he thought it must be someone else—but it was the Ford all right, he could tell by the way it was being driven. He got out a bottle of whisky and slipped it into his pocket. Then he joined Boland at the garage, to see the car safely in—and to read the speedometer. Exactly eleven miles had been registered since Boland's departure. So much, Maguire thought, for Connor's "long way" . . . !

Considering how comparatively little he had learned, he felt absurdly pleased.

"Everything go all right?" he asked.

Boland nodded. "I left it on the step. I didn't feel inclined to disturb them."

"You didn't see my wife ?"

"I didn't see a soul."

"Well, I'm in your debt," Maguire said. He produced the bottle of Irish. "Here you are—and I hope it's to your taste."

"Oh, it will be, I can promise you that. ... Will you not join me in a dram?"

"I don't think I will, thank you," Maguire said. "I've no great liking for the stuff."

"You poor man!" Boland opened the bottle and raised it in the air. "Well—here's to the harp of auld Ireland! May it never lack a string while there's a gut in a policeman!"

He swallowed a mouthful, stoppered the bottle, said, "Good night, Mr. Maguire," and went off humming into the darkness.

Thoughtfully, Maguire returned to the house.

Chapter Eight

It was a few minutes after midnight when Nora got back. Maguire heard the van turn in at the gate and was out in the drive as it pulled up. He opened the doors and helped her down. One glance at her face was enough to tell him that the visit had been satisfactory. Though she looked very tired, her expression was far less strained than it had been, and her smile was unforced. Thankfully, he led the way into the kitchen, where he had some milk and sandwiches ready for her. She sank into a chair with a grateful sigh.

Maguire closed the door. "Well—how are they?"

"They're all right, darling. . . . Oh, I can't tell you how relieved I feel."

"Were they expecting you?"

"Yes, and they were *so* glad to see me, so excited . . . You were quite right, James, they *weren't* snatched away from here and they weren't frightened—they'd been given a sort of explanation, as you thought they would be. Donnelly told me what it was before I went up to them, so things weren't nearly as tricky as I'd expected. I just waited, and let the boys talk, and soon I'd got the whole story from them. . . . It seems that a man named MacEoin called at the house in a car not long after they got back from the tent yesterday and told them you'd asked him to take them away for a day or two, for a holiday. He said you and I were going to be frightfully busy because of what had been found in the tent, which was rather secret, though they'd know all about it in the end. He said you particularly wanted them to go off right away and that their toys and things would be sent on afterwards and that he'd planned a wonderful time for them."

Maguire grunted. "And they believed it all, did they?"

"Well, yes. . . . The thing was, they apparently knew this man MacEoin—he'd been working on the site, on the ancient village, and they'd talked to him a lot and even been allowed to help him sometimes and of course they'd come to like him. So although they weren't too happy about being rushed off without even saying good-bye to us, they did go along with him quite trustingly. And it turned into quite an adventure—they stopped somewhere on the way and MacEoin built a fire and they cooked sausages in a frying-pan and he told them stories. They obviously had a grand time. . . ."

"It all sounds a typical piece of Connor organisation," Maguire said grimly.

"Yes, doesn't it. . . . And then to-day, of course, they got a message quite early that I was coming to see them, so that kept them cheerful."

"Weren't they surprised that you went so late?"

"I think they were more intrigued than surprised—they seemed to take it as part of the adventure. I said I hadn't been able to come earlier because of all the things that were happening—making it sound rather mysterious, the way MacEoin had. It seemed the only thing to do. I said that everything would be over in a few days, and then we'd tell them all about it. . . . And I said I'd try and visit them again—I thought it would help to keep them happy, and maybe I'll be able to. . . ." Nora sighed. "Of course, they don't really like it, it's no good pretending they do—they think it's all very odd, and they're rather disturbed, and Rory cried a bit when I said I had to go—I hated leaving them. But it's so much better than it might have been. . . . At least we know now that they're not actually miserable—I don't think there'll be any lasting effects. And they're certainly being well looked after—they've got a proper bed and warm bedclothes and they're getting plenty to eat, and now of course they've got their own clothes and toys, too."

Maguire nodded. "Well, that's all very reassuring. . . ." He lit his pipe, and puffed for a moment in silence. Then he said, "I don't suppose the boys knew where they'd been taken to, did they?"

"I'm sure they didn't. ..." Nora told him about MacEoin's precautions—how he'd delayed the last part of the journey till after dark, and hadn't told them the truth about where they were. "There were loads of questions I wanted to ask them about the place but Donnelly warned me that if I tried I'd be brought straight back, so of course I didn't dare."

"Oh, well, it was only to be expected," Maguire said. "Connor isn't a man to overlook obvious things like that. ... What did you see of the place yourself?"

"Hardly anything. They covered my eyes as I went in and out, so all I actually saw was the room where the boys were. It was rather small, only about ten feet square, with a low ceiling and a tiny window. It had old-fashioned iron beds and a wooden chair and a table and flowered wall-paper and a piece of matting on the floor. It was very simple—but I think it was clean. ..."

"It sounds like a cottage room."

"I'm sure it was. A quite small cottage, too."

"Is there anything else you can tell me about the place? Think hard!"

"Well—the stairs were short and steep, without any covering on them, and they seemed to go straight up from the front door. And the path to the door was rather grassy."

"Did you have to walk far, or did the van go close to the door?"

"It went quite close—I only had to walk a step or two."

"That sounds as though there might have been a track to the cottage."

"There could have been."

Maguire nodded again. "Now what about the journey, Nora? I suppose you've no idea which way you started off?"

She thought for a moment. "As a matter of fact, I have. ... We went down the hill, turned right at the fork and left at the lane. ... Then I lost track."

"That's not bad. ... And did anything special strike you on the journey? Anything significant?"

"Not a thing. I did listen, but there was nothing much to hear. ... It must have been flat all the way—the driver hardly had to change gear at all, in spite of the van being so old."

"Flat all the way. . . ." Maguire looked interested. "Anything else?"

"I don't think so."

"Was there much traffic?"

"Practically none."

"Did you hear any outside noises—any voices, for instance?"

"No."

"Then it doesn't sound as though you went through any towns—or even villages."

"I'm sure we didn't—not big ones, anyway. I'd have seen the glow of lights through the ventilator in the roof. "We seemed to be driving through completely empty country."

"Did you stop anywhere?"

"No. . . . We didn't even slow down. We just kept going, at about thirty miles an hour—on and on."

"Surely you must have slowed down occasionally . . . ? What about crossing major roads?"

Nora considered. "We didn't, you know—not during the first half-hour, anyway, I went to sleep after that. . . . It seemed a terribly long way."

"Actually," Maguire said, "it was about five miles."

Nora stared at him.

"Five and a half, to be exact. I managed to find out while you were away. . . . It's quite definite."

She looked completely dumbfounded. "You mean all that driving was just to make us think it was a long way?"

"That's right."

"I'd never have thought of it. . . . James, how on earth did you discover?"

"I played a trick on Boland. . . ." He told her how he'd been ordered to go into the house, how it had set him thinking, and about the Teddy-bear and how the speedometer had given the mileage away.

Nora was silent for a moment. Then she said, "That was very clever of you."

Maguire gave a rueful shrug. "You know what they say about necessity ... I Anyway, there it is—the boys are only about five and a half miles away. From your description of the journey, I'd say you were driven round and round more or less in the same place."

"No wonder it was so dull!"

"I'm not sure it was as dull as you think," Maguire said. "I'd like to look at a map. .... Let's go up, shall we?"

"I'm more than ready," Nora said.

In a few moments Maguire joined her in the bedroom with a six-inch map of the district, which he spread out on the bed. For a while he studied it without speaking.

"Yes, it's most interesting," he said at last. "Look here. ...."

Nora bent over it with him.

"This is the way you started off," he said, pointing. "Down the hill, then right, then left. .... That takes you straight into the plain. You say the road was flat all the way, so it looks as though you stayed in the plain. Incidentally, that could be the reason why they sent me indoors—I'd have been able to see you for far too long. ... Now if you'd gone five and a half miles to the north-west or west, you'd have had to cross the Navan-Trim main road—and no one would do that without slowing right down. So it's much more likely you went to the south-west or south. You said you didn't go through any big villages—and that way you wouldn't have had to. You could have kept on round and round this circle of lanes. It's the right sort of empty country—just scattered farm-houses. ... I wonder if one of them could be the place?"

Nora gazed uneasily at the map. "Would it make any difference if we knew?"

"It would be a step forward," Maguire said. "It would give us more freedom of action."

"How would it? You said there was nothing we could do—you said Connor had us in the hollow of his hand."

"I've been thinking about things since then. ... Look, suppose we suddenly found ourselves in a position to get a message through secretly to someone about the plot—to the police, say. As things are, we wouldn't dare to risk it. But if we knew we could tell them at the same time exactly where the children were being held, it would make all the difference. They'd be able to rescue them first, and swoop on Connor afterwards."

"But there's no chance at all that we'd be able to get a message through," Nora said. "Not secretly. How could we, when we're both being watched all the time ?"

"I know that's the position at the moment," Maguire agreed, "and I expect it'll go on—but there's always the possibility that something might change before next Saturday. . . . At least if we knew where the children were we'd be better placed to seize any chance that offered."

"Well," Nora said, "we *don't* know where they are and I wouldn't have thought there was any means of finding out. Even if your guess about the plain is right, they could be in any one of dozens of cottages—and there's no way of discovering which. . . ." She sounded quite firm about it. "Darling, I'm sorry, but I really must go to bed now—I'm absolutely worn out. . . ."

"Of course," Maguire said. "We'll talk about it again to-morrow."

Chapter Nine

He was up before seven next morning. Work on the site hadn't yet begun but he could hear sounds of activity coming from the camp. Looking out, he spotted the hill-side guard, smoking and talking to another man. That meant the other side of the house wasn't being watched for the moment. Without waking Nora, he slipped across the landing to his study and sat down by the window. The day was sunny, and visibility was good. The countryside had a honey-coloured glow in the slanting morning rays. He took a pair of binoculars from the table drawer where he kept his field instruments, and moved his chair nearer to the window, and started to examine the arc of the plain to the south and south-west.

The glasses were powerful, and he was able to pick out farmsteads several miles away without difficulty. But that, he soon realised, was all he could hope to do. Buildings five miles away were much too far off for him to make out any small details, such as a car standing outside or a human figure. Even if one of those distant specks *was* the roof under which the children were living, there was no chance that he would be able to identify it—not from here. Not without some sort of assistance from the place itself. If only, he thought, the boys had had a passion for making smoke signals to each other, instead of digging with trowels! But of course they wouldn't have been allowed to do anything like that, anyway. . . .

A glint of glass caught his eye, and he turned the binoculars on to it. It was coming from the roof of a greenhouse, reflecting the sun, a mile or so away. Interesting! He sat for a while, thinking about reflections. And other things. . . . Slowly, the germ of an idea began to grow in his mind. Maybe there was a way, after all. . . .

He became so engrossed that he scarcely noticed when Nora came in.

"Oh, here you are!" she said. "I couldn't think what had happened to you. . . . I've made the tea. . . ." Her glance fell on the binoculars. "What are you up to?"

He motioned to her to shut the door. "I've just had an idea, Nora."

"Oh?"

"I've thought of a way we might just possibly be able to identify the cottage—always supposing it's out there, and visible."

At once, uneasiness returned to her face. "How . . . ?"

"You were talking last night about trying to arrange another visit. If you could, you might be able to signal to me."

"Signal to you . . . ! But, James, I wouldn't have a chance. They were watching me all the time yesterday. They wouldn't even let me shut the bedroom door. . . ."

"They were being specially careful because they knew you were coming back here," Maguire said. "They had to make sure you didn't find out anything about the place in case we tried to do something about it when you got home . . . But suppose you said you wanted to go and stay with the children till the whole business was over. Then they wouldn't need to take the same precautions."

There was a long pause while Nora considered that.

"I still don't see that I could do anything," she said at last. "They'd hardly fail to notice if I started turning lights on and off, or flashing a torch around."

"A torch isn't the only thing you could flash," Maguire said. "I know this is the longest of long shots, Nora—the cottage may be somewhere else altogether, or it may be hidden by trees, or by a dip in the ground—but there *is* a chance. . . . If you were sitting out of doors in the sun, and you held your handbag mirror at the right angle, and I was watching from here, I'd probably see the reflection."

"What—all that way away?"

"I should think so. You can catch the glitter of the tiniest fragment of glass miles off if the angle's right."

"But I wouldn't know what angle. . . ."

"That isn't difficult. . . . If the cottage was in a place that allowed me an unobstructed view of your mirror from here, you'd obviously be in a position to see Tara Hill, even if you couldn't make out the house itself. . . . Well, you'd hold your mirror in a direction half-way between here and wherever the sun was—that's because light comes off at the angle at which it strikes. You'd have to move it about a little—like this." He demonstrated with a match-box. "If you kept it moving, I'd be pretty sure to catch the flash at some point. And as long as you were careful, no one would suspect anything—you could seem to be feeling for a handkerchief in your bag."

"But how would you know where the flash was coming from . . . ? Even if you did see it, you wouldn't know that—not exactly."

"I'd know the direction it was coming from," Maguire said. "And I'd know the distance by road. I could check it with the map. . . . I think I'd be able to get pretty near it."

"And then what?"

"Then I'd have to see—it would depend entirely on circumstances. I might not be able to do anything at all. But at least I'd be ready if the opportunity came."

"Suppose you tried something, and the plan went wrong . . . ? Suppose Connor found out? You haven't forgotten he said he wouldn't be answerable for the children's safety if either of us tried to give him away."

"I know he said that—and to start with, when we were so upset, I believed him. But now it seems to me that, up to a point, he must be bluffing."

"How can you possibly tell?"

"I've been thinking about it a lot—and I'm pretty sure he is. . . . The thing is, Nora, he needs my co-operation until the Pageant's over. It's absolutely vital to him that I should carry on as though nothing had happened. If I threw in my hand at this stage, everyone would be asking what was wrong, the Press would be down here in droves, his whole plot would be in danger. . . . He knows that. He must know, too, that if he harmed the children he wouldn't have my co-operation any more. There's a sort of balance of interest between us to keep things as they are. . . . I'm not saying he mightn't do something nasty if I *succeeded* in exposing his plot and he was still in a position to take revenge—but if the children had been rescued first he wouldn't be. . . . I certainly don't think he'd upset the balance merely because I'd *failed* to carry out some plan. It wouldn't pay him."

"You don't know. . . . You can't be sure what he'd do."

"At least all the evidence points that way. . . . Look how he's kept us under guard all the time—look how careful he's been to conceal the whereabouts of the cottage from us. That shows the weakness of his position. He knows he can't rely on threats alone—because he knows he's bluffing, and he's afraid we may realise it, too."

"Well, I think it's far too great a risk," Nora said. "I don't think we've the right to gamble with the children's lives."

"Have we the right to let a rising take place without doing everything we can to prevent it?"

"We don't even know that it will take place. . . . Something could easily happen to stop it."

Maguire shook his head. "Nothing's likely to happen now unless it's made to."

"How can you tell . . . ? Anyway, you said yourself the rising would fail."

"Only after a lot of bloodshed. If Connor's men start using sten guns and throwing grenades around, there are bound to be scores of people killed and maimed—maybe hundreds. Good, decent, ordinary people. . . . Innocent people. . . . Haven't we some responsibility to them?"

"Well, yes, but. . ." She broke off, gazing at him piteously. "James, surely one's own children come first . . . ?"

"Of course they do—but not to the point of refusing to take any risk at all, even a tiny one, when there's so much at stake. . . . Nora, how are we going to feel afterwards if we haven't lifted a finger—if we've just waited quietly for the shooting to start? How are we going to feel when we hear about the casualties? How are we going to live with ourselves . . . ? Darling, I'm not suggesting we should do anything rash—but we've got to try and do *something*. And, over the cottage, we have a chance to make a start. It's not a big chance—the heliograph idea may not work, or I may not be able to pinpoint the place, or the cottage may be somewhere else, or I may be so watched that I can't make any move. In fact, it's a pretty slim chance. But it's the only chance we're likely to have, and I think we've got to take it. If it doesn't work out—well, at least we'll have tried."

Nora dropped into the chair by the window. For a long time she sat looking out, saying nothing, fighting her own battle. Maguire waited. He could think of no way to help her. He knew the decision was harder for her than it had been for him. For one thing, he'd had longer to think about it. . . .

She turned at last. Her face was pale—she looked drained by the inward struggle. There was nothing resolute about her, no glow of duty triumphant, nothing but weariness. But when she spoke, the words were brave.

"All right, James—I agree we ought to try. . . . I'll do whatever you say."

Maguire went to her and put his arms around her, pressing his face against her hair. "My love!"

"We must pray that nothing goes wrong."

"Yes."

"I shall hate leaving you."

"I shall hate being without you. . . . But it'll only be for a few days."

"They're going to be such important days, though. I shan't know what's happening, what you're doing. . . . Darling, you will be careful, won't you ?"

"I will—I promise."

"At least the children will be glad—and I'll be glad to be with them. . . . Though we don't even know yet," she added, "that Connor will let me go."

"I can't think why he shouldn't," Maguire said. "After all, he'll be getting another hostage!"

This time it was decided that Nora should make the approach. The exaggerated act that Maguire had put on the first time would hardly work again, since Nora was clearly not beside herself with anxiety any more, But the request would come quite naturally from her. What was more likely than that seeing the children should have increased her desire to be with them?

An opportunity to raise the subject came early. Connor, arriving at the house soon after breakfast with a fresh batch of Pageant problems for Maguire, met Nora at the door.

He smiled at her as though they were established friends. "Well, Mrs. Maguire, I hope you're feeling better this morning. . . . Did you have a good trip?"

"It was a great relief to see the children," she said.

He gave a little nod. "I'm sorry I couldn't take you over myself, but I had rather a lot on my hands. . . . Anyhow, you satisfied yourself the boys were all right?"

"I satisfied myself they were being well looked after, if that's what you mean. . . . They're far from being all right. They're missing me terribly—especially Rory. He was sobbing his heart out when I left—he just doesn't understand. . . . I was thinking—would it make any difference to you if I went and stayed with them till after the Pageant?"

Connor looked surprised. "Would you like to do that?"

"Indeed I would!"

"What about your husband—wouldn't he mind?"

"He says he'd prefer it. I'm afraid I'm more of a worry than a comfort to him while the children are away."

"H'm . . . ! Well, I'm not sure about this. . . . People would be bound to want to know where you'd gone."

"They could be told that my mother was ill in Donegal and that I'd taken the children and gone to look after her. . . . As a matter of fact, Mr. Connor, that would sound much more likely than that I'd sent the children away on their own, when everyone knows they were looking forward so much to the Pageant. I've been wondering how I would explain it to my friends without their thinking it was odd. . . ."

"That's certainly a point. . . ." Connor grinned. "I see you have my interests at heart!"

"I don't want any trouble, that's all."

"Very sensible." For a moment he regarded her in silence. "Well, as I told you, I'm anxious to accommodate you in every way I can. . . . It's a pity you couldn't have suggested it yesterday, though—it would have saved a journey."

"I know—but I was so excited at the prospect of seeing the children I didn't think of anything else."

"You realise you'll have to share that room with them? It's not exactly a palace."

"I'm sure we can manage."

"You won't be allowed much freedom of movement, either. I don't suppose for a moment you'd try to run off with the children while your husband's in my hands. . . ."

"I wouldn't think of it."

"All the same, I prefer not to give you the chance. . . . You'll be expected, of course, to co-operate with your guards in every way—to support the pretence that you're with them voluntarily, if any emergency should arise. . . . For your own safety!"

"I realise that."

"And, naturally, once you've joined the children you won't be allowed to come back and see your husband again in any circumstances whatever. You won't be allowed to see anyone—till after the Pageant."

"I understand. . . . But it's only for a few days."

"True," Connor said. "We must try and have you back for the national rejoicing on the 16th . . . ! All right, Mrs. Maguire, get your things together, and I'll arrange for someone to drive you over at dusk."

For so short a period, there was little to do in the way of preparation. Nora packed her case, and then spent an uneasy morning around the house while Maguire went into Dublin with Connor on Pageant business. Relief that she'd soon be reunited with the children for good was more than offset by her misgivings over what might happen next.

After lunch, in the privacy of the bedroom, Maguire went over the plan with her again. The best time for signalling, he said, would be in the morning, before the angle between the sun and the cottage and the Hill of Tara became too wide. If Connor's demands permitted it, he would be watching from his study window between eleven and twelve each morning. That ought to be good for Nora, too, because it was a time when she could reasonably be outside the cottage, if she was allowed out at all. Maguire showed her once more how to hold and tilt the mirror, and she practised for a while. That was about all they could do. The rest would have to be left to her—and to luck.

Their parting, when the moment came, was brief. Nora looked at him anxiously, earnestly. "You *will* be careful?" she said. "You won't do anything silly."

"I won't," he promised her again. "Trust me, darling."

"I do trust you," she said. "I trust you—and I love you. I don't want anything to happen to you—or to any of us."

He kissed her tenderly. "It won't—you'll see."

A car horn sounded below. Nora said, "There they are—I'd better go."

They went down together to the van. This time Nora was allowed to sit in front with the driver—the overt sign that there was to be no return. Maguire watched her go with a feeling of loss—but also of relief. Already, his mind was preoccupied with the task ahead.

Connor escorted him into the house as the van swung out of the drive—still guarding the secret that was no longer entirely a secret. He, too, seemed relieved that Nora had left. "I think that was quite a good idea, Maguire—it's disturbing to have a woman around in these times of crisis. Now we can really concentrate on the job. No more anxiety. eh?"

"Only about Ireland," Maguire said.

Chapter Ten

That night there was a change in the weather—a temporary one, if the very slight movement of the barometer was any guide, but a sharp disappointment to Maguire when he woke in the morning. From his window he saw that the sky was covered by a layer of high, unbroken cloud. Obviously Nora would have no chance of signalling that day. The best he could do now was to make himself as free as possible for the next day in case conditions improved. He therefore spent a long morning on Pageant affairs with Connor in an effort to clear up all outstanding matters. But he took care that the effort wasn't apparent to Connor—his manner throughout was glum and hostile. The nearer he was to action, the more important it was that he should strike the right note in his behaviour—and the only convincing note was a reluctant acceptance of the inevitable.

The afternoon brought a new sort of strain. Seamus O'Rourke had rung up to say he'd like to have a look at the site, particularly the beehive hut and ancient village, now that everything was nearly ready, and when he arrived just after three Maguire had no choice but to go round with him. Connor went along too.

"You're looking a bit peaky, James," O'Rourke said, as they set off over the Hill. "I expect you'll be glad now when Saturday's over."

"I will indeed," Maguire said, forcing a smile, It was much harder to strike the right note with an observant friend present, as well as a watchful enemy. "It's been a lot of work."

"Maguire's had a bit of domestic upheaval, to add to his other problems," Connor said.

"Oh?—what's happened, James?"

A sentence framed itself in Maguire's mind—a sentence he would have given all he possessed to speak. "This smooth, cunning devil is planning a military rising and he's kidnapped my children to keep me quiet."

He said, "Nora's mother isn't too well—Nora's had to go up to Donegal with the children to look after her for a few days."

"I'm sorry to hear that. She'll be disappointed to miss the Pageant."

"The boys will, too," Maguire said. "But I couldn't have coped with them on my own. As it is, I can manage."

"They could have come and stayed with us, if we'd known. Caithlin would have been glad to have them."

"My suggestion," Connor said, "was that they should stay at the camp—Donnelly's fellows would have looked after them. But I think they wanted to be with their mother."

"Yes—I suppose that's only natural at their age," O'Rourke said.

The dangerous subject passed, as the old man began to concentrate on the site. He was interested in everything, and insisted on making a complete tour. He stumped admiringly round the Banqueting Hall, examined the costumes, asked about the Welcome Board, inspected the "tote" pavilion, and showed understandable pride in the beehive house and village.

"Now that's a fine sight!" he said, beaming at his creation.

Maguire nodded. It was, in fact, a notable exhibit. At considerable cost and immense labour, one of the ancient Kerry cloghans had been superbly reproduced. Its walls were built of sloping stones, skilfully laid without mortar and perfectly arranged to achieve the beehive effect. All the authentic details had been imitated—the sleeping-places cut inside the thickness of the walls; the small hole at the top that served both as chimney and window; the flat upright stone for the door and the large stone for the lintel; the square hole in the floor for cooking. Around the stone cloghan were others, less ambitious and made of wood, but all following established patterns. Enclosing the group was a circular wall of defence. Nearby, the ancient village provided a different and more complete picture. It consisted of round huts, made of stakes with osiers twisted in and out of them, their roofs roughly thatched and their floors strewn with rushes. Some of them had been covered on the outside with white lime to make them more weather-proof. Inside the huts, and on the ground beside them, various objects had been placed to suggest the contemporary way of life—pots for carrying water, jars of honey, apples and onions and other garden produce, candles, pieces of needlework and embroidery, little bags of metal thread for carrying chessmen, hockey sticks, and a variety of tools and weapons. In a thatched chalet nearby, photographs and illustrated booklets offered more detailed documentation for those who would want it.

"It'll be worth the entrance fee on its own," Maguire commented, as the old man completed his inspection. "I congratulate you, Seamus."

O'Rourke twinkled. "Well, I did have a little help, now, with the actual building . . . ! You've got some fine men on the job, Mr. Connor."

Connor smiled. "I agree with you, Mr. O'Rourke."

As they set off back to the entrance, Maguire said, "Shall we be seeing you again before the Pageant, Seamus?"

"I don't expect so," O'Rourke told him. "I'll be conserving my strength for the great day."

Maguire nodded. He felt almost thankful. It had been a gruelling afternoon.

The skies cleared during the night and the day broke fine and sunny, with the prospect of heat later. It was the perfect morning for anyone to spend in a garden—and a promising one for heliography. Maguire was prepared to plead indisposition if necessary in order to be at the house at the right time, but as things turned out the need didn't arise. Connor was in an affable mood when he came to confer. He volunteered the news that Nora and the children were in excellent health and spirits, contented himself with a mere token inspection of the site in Maguire's company, and raised no objection when he said he'd like to catch up with his correspondence. By eleven, Maguire was sitting at his study table and gazing out over the plain, his binoculars handy in an open drawer beside him. With luck, he should have an undisturbed hour.

He still had only the slenderest hope that anything would come of his idea. So many things could go wrong—and just one would be enough. . . . Nora's guards might well insist that she stay out of sight in the cottage. The garden, if there was one, might be shut in, with no view across to Tara. Nora might not get the angle right—or he might not pick up the flash. Considering all the uncertainties, it was really a pretty crazy idea. . . . But not entirely crazy. A second look at the map had made him feel even more strongly that the cottage must be out there somewhere. And Nora was resourceful and reliable. She would do all she could. . . .

He continued to scan the plain, swivelling his eyes constantly from one end of the arc to the other. Until he had something to focus on, binoculars would merely reduce his field of vision. He sat for ten minutes, almost motionless, in intense concentration. Once for a second, his heart gave a leap as something sparkled in the middle distance. He grabbed the glasses—but by the time he'd trained them the reflection had gone. All he could see now was a slowly moving car. Probably it was the car windscreen that had caught the sun. . . . Anyway, the cottage would have been farther away than that.

He had just replaced the glasses when the telephone rang. For a moment he hesitated. If he left the study now he might miss his chance. But if he ignored the phone the guard would be sure to come up. . . . He went down quickly to answer it. It was the Vice-President's private secretary, with a query about the arrangements for the Pageant opening. Maguire dealt briskly with the point, while the man at the table listened, fingering the gun in his pocket. In sixty seconds, the matter was disposed of. Maguire returned to the study.

He had hardly settled back in his chair when his eye was caught by another flash. It was the merest point of light and it lasted only for a fraction of a second. Once more it had gone before he could train the glasses. But after a moment he saw it again, and this time he managed to focus on it. It looked much brighter through the glasses, but he couldn't identify it. It was a long way away, over in the south-west. There seemed to be a group of trees around it. It came, and went, and came again. Excitement rose in Maguire. It was definitely not a motionless object, like a bottle on the ground. But its position wasn't changing—so it wasn't a second car, either. He reached in the table drawer for the hand-bearing compass he used in his field work and took a sight on the flash. It was bearing 232 degrees. For a while he lost it—then there were four more flashes, in quick succession. Now he had no doubts. He checked the bearing again, and made it approximately the same. He waited, but there were no more signals.

He got out the six-inch map and laid a ruler as nearly as he could along a bearing of 232 degrees from Tara Hill. The line passed close to a number of habitations at about the right distance away. He studied the network of lanes. It was reasonable to suppose that Boland, on the night of his trip with the bear, would have taken the shortest possible route—if only to get back to the whisky. With another of his instruments—a wheeled affair made for measuring map distances—Maguire ran off five and a half miles along the map lanes in a south-westerly direction, choosing the most direct way. Within a quarter of a mile of where he stopped, the map showed a small dwelling, almost on the bearing line. No other habitation lay near it. He took a pencil and triumphantly ringed it. It looked, after all, as though his idea might have worked.

His feeling of elation was short-lived. As soon as he began to consider the next step, he saw how limited his progress had been. The margin of error in the method he'd used was far too great for him to be *certain* that the building he'd ringed was the right one. And if it wasn't, he could be heading for frightful dangers. It was unthinkable that he should disclose Connor's plot to anyone until he had first identified the cottage positively and could say with assurance to a rescue party, "That's where you'll find the family."

How could he make sure? There was only one absolutely reliable way he could think of—and that was to go and look. If he could personally satisfy himself by a visit, he'd be in a position—if he dared—to go on from there and contact the authorities. But what likelihood was there that such a chance would arise? He'd been thinking up to now that some momentary weakening of vigilance at the site might give him enough time to disclose the basic plot and the whereabouts of the family to some suitable person. Ten minutes alone at the telephone would suffice. But if he had first to check up personally on the cottage, he would need hours of freedom. There wasn't a hope that he'd be allowed that. . . .

Was there any chance, he wondered, of organising it himself—by eluding his guards? Clearly, he couldn't expect to do that in the day-time—but what about at night? Was it possible that he could get out of the house unnoticed after dark?

He considered the idea sombrely. It was one thing to pit his brains against Connor's in the comparative sanctuary of his study; it was quite another to start climbing out of windows at night. A desert of unknown territory suddenly stretched ahead of him—the world of dangerous physical action. He wasn't equipped for it. He hadn't the temperament. Yet if it was the only way. . . .

He continued to think about it. Suppose he *could* get out of the house unseen . . . ? He would want to reach the cottage as quickly as possible, to cut down the time when his absence might be discovered. He certainly couldn't use the car—the noise would alert the guards at once. He might be able to use Nora's bicycle, though. That would be quiet enough—and it would get him to the cottage in twenty minutes, compared with the hour or so it would take if he walked. Once there, it shouldn't be too difficult to find out if it was the right place, even at night. There would probably be something to tell him—the van, maybe, or a car that he recognised, or a familiar garment on a clothes-line, or even a voice, a sound from the bedroom. . . . If he found that it *was* the right place, he could cycle to a telephone box, ring up Patrick Dillon, the Chief of Police, whom he knew, and quickly tell his story. In an hour, or less, Dillon's men would be at the cottage. . . . If he found it was the wrong place, he could return to Tara with no harm done.

What about the dangers? What about his promise to Nora that

he'd do nothing rash? Was this rash? Soberly, he tried to calculate the risks.

He might, of course, be caught—that was a very real possibility. He might be caught trying to leave the house, or reconnoitring the cottage, or trying to get back into the house if the cottage turned out to be the wrong one. In that event, Connor would undoubtedly be most unpleasant—but his plot would still be undisclosed, he would still need co-operation. Maguire felt that his earlier assessment remained valid—there would be no serious reprisals if he failed.

What if his absence was discovered while he was away? What would Connor think he was doing? He certainly wouldn't suspect him of going to the cottage, after the precautions he'd taken. He would hardly suspect him of going to the police, with the family still hostages in an unknown place. He might well hesitate before doing anything. And with the help of the bicycle, the whole enterprise, from leaving the house to getting the family rescued shouldn't take more than a couple of hours at the outside. Was it likely that the guards would bother to check on Maguire's presence in the house during those two hours? He didn't think so. As far as he knew, they never had.

What about the actual rescue of the family—the police operation? Maguire couldn't believe that the guards would dare to do anything to Nora and the children then. They would know the game was up—they wouldn't want to make things worse for themselves. Probably they wouldn't even have the opportunity to do anything. Dillon should be able to make sure of that. They'd be taken by surprise in the ground-floor room and overwhelmed before they could move. . . .

And, of course, if the plan came off, not only would the family be safe but the plot would be frustrated too. Connor, also, would be taken by surprise. The men in the camp would be rounded up before they had time to uncover their buried weapons. They might not even resist. Once the plot was revealed, they would know they had no hope of success.

Maguire continued to weigh the pros and cons. The slim chance that he might pull something off against the far greater probability of failure. The slight risk to the family, the larger risk that he himself might break his neck or be shot down by some trigger-happy guard, against the certainty of carnage on the 15th if he did nothing.

All through the afternoon he wrestled with himself, with his doubts and his fears. . . . Not until the evening did he finally decide that, if circumstances seemed favourable, he would make the attempt.

The two men who took over guard duty at six o'clock had both been on the night-shift several times before. One, a Dubliner named Waugh, had shown from the beginning an unusual antipathy to Maguire—and the feeling was mutual. Waugh had the face of a vicious bruiser and Maguire felt sure he had the disposition of one, too. He was on the outside watch. The other was a mason from Limerick, a man named Hearne, who had helped to build the ancient village. Hearne was quite amiable, and was taking his duties much more light-heartedly than he had done a day or two before. Maguire had noticed the same tendency in others. It was possible, he thought, that Connor had decided there was less need for stringency, now that he had Nora in his keeping, too, and Maguire himself appeared to have accepted the situation. If so, it might make all the difference to the night's events.

Hearne settled down at the telephone, and was soon sunk in a paper-backed book. Later on in the night, if he followed his usual procedure, he would go into the sitting-room and stretch out on the settee, leaving the door into the hall open. . . . Waugh took up his position on the hill-side at the point where he could watch both front and back entrances. If he also followed custom, he would make an occasional circuit round the outside of the house during the night. It was something that had to be reckoned with.

By now, Maguire had begun to make his plans. He would aim to leave, he thought, about one in the morning. That would be early enough to give plenty of time for the operation to be completed before dawn, and late enough to rule out any disturbing visit by Connor. He would leave by the study window. The study was on the side of the house away from the outside guard. It also had a single bed in it which he occasionally used, and which he would appear to be using to-night. He would knot the bed sheets into some sort of rope and make it fast to a cold water pipe that ran along the wall, and somehow scramble down it. He would then toss the rope back through the window by its free end, so that there would be no danger of the patrolling guard spotting it.

The return trip, in case he had to make it, would be by a downstairs window. Even if it had been safe to leave the rope hanging, he couldn't have climbed it. He would come in, he thought, by the kitchen window. It would mean creeping through the hall to the stairs without alerting Hearne in the sitting-room, but with care it should be possible. ... Anyway, he wasn't feeling too concerned about the route back. He had been examining the map again and had noticed that the approach to the building he had ringed was by a short track from a lane. It could well be a grassy track, which tallied with Nora's description after her first visit. The odds on his having picked the right place had improved. ...

The weather that evening was hot and close, which helped his plan considerably. It was natural that he should open the bottom of his study window wide on such a night, and leave it open. It was natural that he should leave the kitchen window open a little. It was natural, too, that shortly before dusk he should take a gentle stroll up and down the drive. ... Waugh, on the hill-side, made a move in his direction as he went into the garage, but a move with no sort of urgency about it. Maguire had plenty of time to shift Nora's bicycle, unobserved, to a position near the door where he'd be able to get at it quietly and easily later. He was also able to check that the tyres were pumped up.

On his way back into the house he stopped in the hall for a few words with Hearne. He would be working late that night, he said—it was too hot to sleep. He hoped his movements wouldn't disturb anyone. Hearne grinned. "I won't be sleeping either, Mr. Maguire," he said. "You can make all the rumpus you want." Maguire nodded, and went up to his study.

Behind a locked door, he made his final preparations. He stripped the sheets from the bed and carefully knotted them together. He changed into a maroon shirt, dark grey trousers and a dark jacket, to make himself as inconspicuous as possible out of doors. He put on a pair of rubber-soled shoes. He checked over the things he must take with him—the map with the marked house on it, a small torch, some coins for the telephone box. He didn't think he'd forgotten anything. He sat down to wait.

It was a nerve-racking wait. He felt keyed up now, and impatient to start. But a plan was a plan. Beyond pacing around a little for the benefit of Hearne below, he made no move till well after twelve. Then, as the clock in the hall struck the half-hour, he seated himself at the table as though he were working and started to watch from the window. After about twenty minutes he saw Waugh come into view, making his round of the house. Maguire bent over the table, pretending to be absorbed in a book, listening to the guard's footsteps, his slow retreat back to the hill-side.

Zero hour!

Maguire moved quickly now. One end of the knotted sheet was already made fast to the water pipe. He dropped the other end out of the window, switched off the room light, and climbed out on to the sill, grasping the rope. He was a heavy man, but the sheets were almost new. He prayed that they would hold. It would be too bad if they didn't, for the distance to the ground was more than twelve feet. For a second, he stayed listening. Then, very cautiously, he lowered himself over the sill. He felt something give as the strain came on the improvised rope—but nothing broke. He went down rapidly, hand over hand. It was easier than he'd expected. A moment later his feet were on the ground. He gathered up the bottom of the sheet and knotted it over and over round itself till its end was a tight ball at the level of his shoulder. Then, poised on his toes, he flung the ball back through the window. For a sickening moment he thought that a loop was going to be left hanging out over the sill—but the weight of the ball drew it in, and the rope vanished. The ball had landed with a slight thump, but Hearne must be used to odd noises from the study by now. Maguire stepped quickly on to the grass beside the path and crept silently along it till he reached the garage.

He lifted the bicycle out without a sound and, still keeping to the grass verge, carried it down the drive to the gate. Behind him, all was quiet. He could hardly believe it. He'd escaped from the house!—a feat that a couple of days ago he'd have thought himself quite incapable of. The worst hazard of all seemed to be safely past. With new confidence, he squeezed himself on to the saddle of the bicycle and free-wheeled away down the hill.

Chapter Eleven

There was no moon, but the night was bright with stars, and he rode without a lamp. A cyclist in these parts at one o'clock in the morning must be a very rare thing—and a lamp would be visible from Tara for miles. It seemed better not to attract any attention to himself.

Once he was away from the house and out on to the flat plain, he didn't hurry. For one thing, the bicycle was awkwardly small for him, the saddle far too low, so that his knees jack-knifed out sideways as he pedalled. Also, he wanted to arrive cool and composed at the cottage, not in a sweat.

He had memorised the earlier turnings, and he made steady progress for three miles. Then, at a fork, he had to stop and consult the map again, shielding the torch with his hand. Left, left—and right. . . . That should bring him to the place. He pedalled on. Once or twice he passed a roadside farm-house, its roof looming against the stars. Once a dog barked as he whirred by. But he met no one on the road, and saw no lights. The countryside was asleep.

At a point about fifty yards from the marked house he dismounted and stuck the bicycle under a hedge. It would be safer to cover the last bit on foot. He went forward slowly, with infinite care. That barking dog had worried him. Suppose there was a dog at the cottage? It was something he hadn't thought of— and a real danger. However carefully he moved it was impossible not to make some noise. The lane was roughly surfaced, and small stones grated underfoot in spite of his rubber soles. His heart was beginning to hammer. Why had he ever supposed that getting away from Tara was the most difficult part of the trip?

He was almost there now. In a moment the approach track opened on his left and he turned into it. He was relieved to find there was no gate. The going became better—on the grassy earth his steps made no sound at all. He inched his way forward. The track curved to the right after a few yards, and as he rounded the bend he saw the cottage. It lay at the foot of what seemed to be a little knoll, with some trees close by. No lights showed in the windows.

He stood motionless, listening. He couldn't hear anything except the rustle of leaves. He couldn't see much, either. He took a couple of cautious steps—and a twig snapped underfoot. In the silence, it sounded like a gunshot. He held his breath. . . . Nothing happened. At least he knew now that there wasn't a dog. He crept forward again. He was nearly up to the cottage. There was no van or car outside. He stopped opposite the door. It was a very small cottage—one room up and one down, by the look of it. Just the sort Nora had described. . . . Then his spirits sagged, as he saw that all the windows were shut. No one would sleep behind closed windows on a hot night like this. The place must be empty. It couldn't be the right house, after all. . . .

With less caution, now, he walked round to the back. There was no sign of life—no sign, even, of recent habitation. He went to the front again and peered through the window. He could just make out a stick or two of furniture, but nothing else. He shone his torch through the glass, without much effect. He tried the front door. It was locked—but as he put his weight against it the ancient lock gave way and the door swung in. He shone his torch around the room. A chair or two, a rough table with a couple of bottles on it, some worn linoleum on the floor, a pile of litter. . . .

Suddenly he caught his breath. From the pile he picked out what looked like a handful of yellow flock. He'd seen that before—he couldn't doubt what it was. Stuffing from Rory's Teddy-bear . . . !

So they *had* been here—this *was* the place. He climbed the short, steep stairs to the upper room to make quite sure. Flowered wall-paper, iron bedsteads, a strip of matting on the boards. . . . Yes, there'd been nothing wrong with his calculations, with his direction-finding. He was too late, that was all. The bedding had gone, the suitcases—everything of importance. The family must have been moved to some other place—and, by the look of things, they wouldn't be coming back.

It was a crushing disappointment after all the effort, all the planning, all the hopes. But Maguire wasted no time in vain regrets. He had done his best, and he had failed. As things were, there could be no question of ringing the police. All he could hope to do now was get back into his own house undetected. He left the cottage, closing the door behind him, and walked quickly back to the lane. In a few seconds he had found the bicycle and was pedalling off the way he had come.

He rode much faster on the return journey. In fifteen minutes he was at the foot of Tara Hill. He dismounted there, and pushed the bicycle up to the gate. The house, he noted with relief, was dark and quiet. There had been no alarm. He carried the bicycle along the grass verge to the garage and restored it to its place. Then he crept round to the back of the house, alert for any sign or sound of Waugh. It would be horrible to run into that brute in the darkness. He negotiated a corner, and peered ahead. The guard was in his old spot on the hill-side, his head silhouetted against the sky. . . .

Maguire waited. He knew he couldn't hope to climb through the kitchen window undetected until Waugh went off on his round. He stood back in the shadow of the angled wall, trying to control his nervous excitement. . . .

He had to wait for nearly half an hour. Then Waugh got to his feet, and stretched, and started to stroll down towards the house. At first he seemed to be coming straight for Maguire, who prepared to retreat. Then he suddenly changed direction and disappeared round the front.

Maguire moved quickly to the kitchen window. With relief, he saw that it was still open. He wished, now, that he'd opened it wider and left himself more room—but at the time he hadn't really expected he'd have to use it. It was going to be a tight squeeze. . . . He grabbed the sill and with difficulty hoisted himself up, his feet scrabbling for a purchase against the brick. . . . Good!—he'd made it! And without too much noise. He looked through the window. The kitchen door was closed—so he ought to be all right. Now he had to get his body through the gap—and without pushing the window up. These sash windows made a shocking row when they were raised. He got his head through, his shoulders. . . . He was contorted now like an acrobat. He paused to rest, to get his breath. . . . At that moment he heard a step on the path to the right. Waugh was coming round the house. Now it was a case of the devil and the deep blue sea. He *must* get through. It was a question of seconds. . . . He gave a great lurch, grabbed the edge of the draining board inside, pulled himself in. . . . He'd done it . . . ! Then something fell to the floor with a fearful crash.

He stood petrified. Already there was a step in the hall. He couldn't retreat, he couldn't advance. The kitchen door flew open, a switch clicked, the room was a blaze of light. Hearne was in the doorway, a gun in his hand. His face was pale, a little scared. He looked at the open window, and at Maguire. There was nothing amiable about him now.

"And what would you be doing here, Mr. Maguire? What is it you're up to?"

Maguire said nothing. He was wondering what he *would* say.

Hearne, still covering him, unlocked the back door and called, "Patrick . . . !" Then he turned to Maguire again. "Into the sitting-room with you!" he said, "We'll see what the Captain has to say about this."

Chapter Twelve

Maguire stood with his back to the wall in the sitting-room, waiting for Connor to speak. Waugh stood close by, his gun held menacingly at the ready. Both guards had made their reports. Regan, the foreman, was inspecting the knotted sheet that had been brought down, from the study. Connor, seated at a small table with Donnelly beside him, was studying the map that Hearne had found in Maguire's pocket.

For the first time, Connor really looked to Maguire like the ruthless leader of a bloody enterprise. Every trace of friendliness and consideration had vanished. His thin lips no longer wore their faintly sardonic smile. He had the implacable air of a hanging judge. In view of the fact that his plot had plainly not been endangered, Maguire thought his attitude extreme.

"So that was where you went," Connor said, looking up at last. "To the house you've marked."

Maguire nodded. There seemed no point in denying it.

"Why did you go?"

"I thought my family might be there. I wanted to make sure."

"And if they had been, I suppose you'd have gone to the police afterwards? To inform on us."

"I hadn't any plans," Maguire said. At least he needn't admit anything beyond the evidence. "I wanted to see if they were there, that's all."

"You expect me to believe that?"

"It's your affair what you believe," Maguire said. "I'd have thought it was quite natural for a man in my position to try and find out where his family was."

Connor leaned forward, tapping the map. "Who told you this was the house?"

"No one told me. I worked it out for myself."

"And how did you manage that, I'd like to know?"

Maguire hesitated—but only for a second. His communications with Nora were finally cut—there was no hope that he'd be able to use the heliograph method a second time.

"My wife told me about the route the van took," he said. "She told me it went down the hill first of all, and then stayed on the flat all the time. I looked at the map, and I thought the house must be somewhere out there on the plain. I arranged with her that when she went the second time she should try to signal with her mirror—and she did."

For a long moment, Connor just stared at him. Then he said, "You've a lively invention, Maguire—too lively. . . . I don't think I've ever heard a more unlikely story."

"It happens to be true."

"You saw a signal, and immediately you were sure which house it was coming from?—sure enough to draw a ring round the place!"

"I wasn't sure," Maguire said. "I told you—I was going to *make* sure. . . . Anyway, I'd taken a bearing on it. . . ."

"A bearing! Imagine . . . ! Tell me, Maguire, what made you think the cottage was within signalling distance in the first place. You'll remember the journey took your wife nearly an hour."

Maguire was on the point of telling him—but then decided not to. He had no duty to any of these gunmen, even to Boland—but Boland had done him a good turn and he'd no desire to get him into trouble.

"I found out," he said.

Connor nodded grimly. "You found out, all right—because someone told you. You found out because someone who knew marked the place for you on the map. You couldn't have done it any other way. You surely don't imagine I believe that signalling nonsense. . . . Who told you, Maguire? *Who told you?*"

"No one told me," Maguire said. "I discovered it for myself. That's the truth."

Connor pushed back his chair and strode over to the wall. His face was dark with anger, his fists clenched. Maguire braced himself for a rain of blows. But they didn't come. Instead, Connor gave a shrug. "I could make you talk, Maguire—easily—but I don't think it'll be necessary. I shall soon discover the truth. . . ." He motioned to Donnelly and Regan, and without another word the three of them left the room.

Hearne followed them into the hall and stayed there. Waugh lit a cigarette, flicked the match on to the carpet, and moved scowling to the window. Maguire stood uncertainly, dabbing the sweat from his forehead. Connor's abrupt departure had come as a complete anticlimax. He had no idea what was going to happen next, what he was expected to do. Maybe nothing would happen for quite a while. . . . Neither of the guards spoke. The minutes passed. Maguire glanced at his watch. The time was a quarter past four.

He turned to Waugh. "Is there any reason why I shouldn't go to bed?" he asked.

"Waugh gave him a look of unbelievable venom. "You can go to hell, Mr. Maguire, for all I care."

Maguire returned the look, coldly, and went upstairs to the bedroom.

He threw off his jacket and lay down on one of the beds without bothering to undress further. He felt worn out after the night's exertions and the strain of the tribunal-like scene below, but he knew there would be no sleep for him yet. His mind was far too active.

He still felt chagrined over the failure of a plan that might so easily have succeeded. He wished now that he hadn't been so foolish as to mark the house on the map, and so open the way to a lot of futile argument. He was a little disturbed by Connor's behaviour in the sitting-room. But he felt no desperate anxiety about the immediate future.

It was true that Connor's manner could hardly have been more threatening—but it was significant that at the crucial moment he'd refrained from physical violence. He must have realised, of course, that the basic position hadn't changed. With the failure of the counter-plan, the old balance of interest had been restored. Connor was in a temper now, a suspicious temper, but his inquiries would get him nowhere and he'd have to accept in the end that Maguire had been telling him the truth about the signalling. He'd cool off then, if only to get his prisoner back in the Pageant facade. . . . That, at any rate, was how Maguire read the situation.

On a longer view, the outlook was as black as ever. Worse . . . ! For now that the family had been moved to an unknown place and all contact with Nora broken, there was no hope at all of frustrating the rising in safety. . . . But as Maguire started to think of that, his concentration blurred. He'd been over the ground so often. . . .

He drifted gradually into an uneasy half-world between dozing and waking. It was during one of his waking periods that he was startled by the sound of a shot. A single shot, from somewhere up on the hillside. He got up and looked out of the window. The sky in the east was grey with the coming dawn. The time was a quarter past five. He stood there for a while, frowning. The shot must have been accidental—a careless guard. . . .

He was about to turn away when he saw two men hurrying down the hill-side. They were carrying something. It looked like an improvised stretcher. It *was* a stretcher. Behind them another man appeared, with a pick and shovel over his shoulder. . . . Now Maguire could see that there was someone on the stretcher—a man whose head lolled lifelessly with every movement. The group sheered away before it reached the house—but not before Maguire had recognised the dead man.

It was Boland!

Sick with horror and foreboding, Maguire waited for Connor's next move. He hadn't long to wait. It was just after six when he heard voices downstairs. A moment later Connor came up—alone. He looked greyer than the dawn.

Maguire faced him in bitter anger. "You had Boland shot!"

Connor shook his head. "You're wrong, Maguire. . . . I shot him myself. I wouldn't be a leader for long if I left it to others to do the unpleasant jobs."

"You—*murderer!*"

"I had no choice," Connor said. He sat down on the bed. "Believe me, I didn't like doing it. But it was the decision of the court martial—and the right decision."

"Boland did nothing," Maguire shouted at him. "Nothing to deserve that. Mother of God, why didn't I tell you the truth before ...? He took a toy to my children, that's all. I tricked him—I let him have my car and I read the mileage on the speedometer. That's how I knew where to look for the cottage. Don't you understand, Connor—you've killed a man for nothing. It was an act of kindness. ..."

"It was an act of weakness," Connor said, "an act of treachery. ... I know exactly what happened. Boland admitted everything. You persuaded him to take your toy and you gave him a bottle of whisky."

"He'd have gone anyway."

"But he took the whisky. You don't know it, Maguire, but spirits are banned from this camp. They were banned when Boland made an error of judgment once before—because of whisky. I overlooked that. I gave him a second chance. I ought to have been shot myself for taking the risk. I should have known that he was unreliable, that he'd do anything for whisky. Even to telling you a vital secret and imperilling our whole undertaking."

"He didn't tell me a vital secret. He didn't tell me anything."

"Of course he did. In return for the whisky, he told you where the cottage was. He showed you on the map."

"If he admitted that," Maguire said, "you must have treated him so abominably that he didn't know what he was saying."

"He didn't admit that. He still hoped to save his skin. But he admitted all the rest—and the conclusion was inevitable. The court was satisfied that you couldn't have discovered the whereabouts of the cottage in any other way."

"The *court* ...! Connor, the man's dead—what I say now can neither save him nor destroy him. I'm telling you the truth—all he did was take the toy. You've innocent blood on your hands."

"If I had," Connor said grimly, "it wouldn't be the first time. As I told you, we're at war. But in Boland's case, it isn't so. I just don't believe you, Maguire. You've got a good line in talk but it's wasted on me. You see, I understand your motive. You're doing what Boland did—you're lying to try and save *your* skin. You won't admit that you bribed one of my men to betray a secret because you're afraid of what I'll do to you."

Maguire gave a weary sigh. "Have it your own way—your mind's obviously closed. ... Anyway, what *are* you going to do to me?"

"Ah!" Connor got up and took a turn round the room. "I've naturally been thinking hard about that. After what you've done, I'd certainly have no compunction about shooting you. It would be a very popular move in the camp, I may say. The men hold you responsible for Boland's death. ... But I can't do it. I still need your co-operation for three days. So I'm not going to harm you. I'm going to let you continue with your work—*our* work ... ! This time, though, I intend to leave no loopholes. I underrated your resourcefulness before. I underrated your recklessness. You almost got the better of me—and that's something I'm not used to. Well, I can assure you it won't happen again. ..."

He paused, as though ordering his thoughts. Then he said, "In the first place, you will be kept from now on under the closest twenty-four hour surveillance. You will see no one except in my company, and you will not be allowed to move around the camp without me. That should make it physically impossible for you to do any more secret plotting. ... If you are caught attempting to do so, or if you give inadequate co-operation or disobey any instructions, I shall order that your family be kept without food and water until the Pageant is over. ... Is that clear?"

Maguire gave a dejected nod.

"You see, I am graduating the penalties ... ! Of course, it will still be open to you to blurt out what you know when we are in public together—but before anyone could grasp what you were talking about, I and my men would have escaped. We should then have nothing to lose, and in reprisal we should kill your wife and children. You know me well enough by now to realise that this is not an idle threat. Make no mistake—we should do it. . . ."

He paused again.

"And, just in case you should think there might still be some way out for you, I am making new arrangements about the family. I am going to have them moved to yet another place, a very remote one. I am going to put them in the charge of two of my toughest men—men who under different names are already wanted for what you and the authorities would call 'murder.' Only they, and I, will know where the place is. And they will have their instructions. . . . You will see, therefore, that if you should step out of line the blow would fall long before you could do anything about it. . . . And that, I think, just about takes care of everything."

Chapter Thirteen

Far away in the heart of Ireland, Nora was looking back with a mixture of regret and relief at the things that had happened to her in the past two days.

At first, everything had gone as James had hoped it would. The van had taken only a few minutes to reach the cottage on its second journey, and even in the dark Nora had seen enough of the route to realise that the place was roughly where he'd thought it might be. She had pretended suitable amazement to the driver and the guards that it was so near Tara after all.

The children had been overjoyed when she'd told them she'd come to stay with them until after the Pageant. She had easily parried their questions about why they had to be in such a tiny house, with MacEoin and the other man, Kiernan, sleeping on the floor downstairs and themselves crowded into the bedroom without sufficient beds. Daddy had had to arrange it all in a great hurry, she'd said, and Daddy would explain everything later. Meanwhile, they must all get along as best they could.

Though the first morning had been too cloudy for signalling, she hadn't wasted it. The children, she'd quickly learned, had been allowed to play on the secluded piece of rough grass at the back of the house. If they could go out there, she'd said, obviously she must be allowed to as well, or they'd think it very strange. Anyway, she'd be stifled if she had to stay in the tiny cottage all the time. MacEoin had said, yes, she could use the garden, provided he or Kiernan was out there too. No chances were to be taken, evidently, of her slipping away with the children, in spite of Connor's apparent confidence that she wouldn't try. But the concession had been enough. At the first opportunity she had gone out to reconnoitre, and had discovered at once that the place had signalling possibilities. It wasn't in a hollow, and it wasn't shielded by the clump of trees. A little way up the knoll she had found a spot from which, looking north-east, she could clearly see the Hill of Tara—and it was a spot that the early sun would shine on, if there was any. Again, James's hopes had been realised.

The day had slipped by remarkably quickly. It had been impossible for Nora to put out of her mind the dark events that were building up at Tara, but she'd been sufficiently occupied not to dwell on them all the time. She had done her best to clean up the squalid cottage, with Kiernan's help, and had cooked the. food that MacEoin had brought in. The atmosphere of a camping holiday had been maintained. The boys had rigged up a rough-and-ready wigwam in the garden with the help of a couple of rugs and some old sacks, and had amused themselves without difficulty. A messenger had come to the cottage after dark, and stayed for a while, but there had been no other callers. At night, Nora had shared Rory's bed, and slept fitfully.

The next morning had been the sunny one and Nora, not without trepidation, had flashed her signal. Actually, it had been much easier than she'd expected She had gone up the slope with a book just after eleven, leaving the boys with Kiernan at the wigwam. She had settled down on the grass and pretended to read. After a moment or two she had opened her handbag and carried out James's instructions. No one had taken any notice of her and she had flashed for several minutes. Then Rory had joined her with Kiernan, and she'd had to stop.

She had spent a preoccupied afternoon, wondering whether James had received the signal, whether he would really be able to pinpoint the cottage, and—the nagging, ever-present uneasiness—what he would do about it. ... Then, suddenly, everything had changed. Regan had arrived in a car, with fresh instructions. They were all to move on that evening, to a new place. Connor had decided that the cottage, though convenient up to now, was too near to Tara to be a safe hide-out over the busy Pageant period, when a lot more people would be using the lanes. That, at any rate, was what Nora had gathered from the scraps of talk she'd overheard. There had been nothing she could do about it, even if she'd wanted to. She had packed up, and at dusk another car had come and they'd started a journey that had lasted much of the night.

Now here they were, early in the morning, in the wildest and most isolated spot that Nora had ever seen. The building they'd been brought to was even more broken-down and derelict than the cottage had been, and certainly no bigger. It had been a shepherd's shack, MacEoin told her—one of several, he added with a grin, that Mr. Connor had acquired in strategic spots for use during his organisation's training period. He wouldn't say where the place was, only that it was a long way from Dublin—which this time Nora believed. The country was beautiful and empty and very high. All around were pointed mountains, blue at the peaks and tawny in the valleys. There was a rough cart track to the shack itself, up which the car had laboured, but there wasn't a road or even another path visible, except those that the sheep had made for themselves up the heather-covered slopes. On every side there was nothing but folded hills and rocky moorland and streams and little shining loughs.

The children were entranced when they woke and discovered where they were. The day was sunny, the air delicious, the hills inviting—and with all the wonderful possibilities outside, the discomfort of the tiny shack didn't bother them at all. This was going to be a *real* holiday. With whoops of glee, they rushed around, exploring. Then, after breakfast, MacEoin took them down to one of the lakes to try and catch some fish with an improvised rod and line. Nora sat nearby on the bank, with wild pansies all about her and gorgeous yellow irises at her feet, thinking how James would have loved this place if they could have been there together with no anxieties, and wondering what he was doing. She hoped now that he *hadn't* received her signal the previous day, since anything he attempted could only be fruitless. ... She was glad, though, that she'd agreed to signal, that she'd actually done it. No one would be able to say now that they hadn't tried. ... And

107

maybe, after all, something *would* happen to prevent the rising taking place. It was harder than ever to believe in it, in this lovely spot. . . .

The sound of a car on the track behind her made her turn. It was Kiernan, who had been down in the valley all the morning, laying in stores. She watched him park the car at the head of the lake and come walking along the bank towards her. He was walking quickly, and beckoning to MacEoin, as though he had news. His face, as he approached, looked hard and set. "Your husband's been giving trouble," he threw out, as he passed Nora. "MacEoin and I are going back to-night. . . . You'll be getting a couple of new guards. . . ."

Chapter Fourteen

Maguire was sitting at the table in his study. In front of him was the message he was expected to translate into Irish and Ogham for the Board of Welcome. Across the room, a guard was stretched out on the bed, reading a newspaper.

The translation, Connor had said brusquely that morning, should have been finished long ago. With the Pageant only a couple of days away, there would scarcely be time to get the Board inscribed and the paint dry. The text must be ready without fail by noon at the latest. . . . Maguire, with Connor's threats still fresh in his mind, had been in no position to refuse. Yet his thoughts were all of other things. . . .

The execution of Boland had had a profound effect upon him. It had left him not only appalled by the act, but bewildered about Connor. He could understand that in the context of planned rebellion a deliberate and proved informer would be shown no mercy. Dreamers were ruthless people; romantic Irish patriots had never hesitated to shed the blood of former comrades caught in betrayal. But even Connor hadn't accused Boland of deliberate betrayal; only of weakness leading to dangerous disclosure. And the evidence had been derisory, the trial a mockery. It seemed almost as though Connor must have had some other motive for his act of terror, beyond a wish to protect his cause. The need to prove something to his men—or to himself? The need to demonstrate his life-and-death authority? There had been something almost pathological in this hasty killing.

Maguire found himself going back over his earlier encounters with Connor, over conversations they had had, seeking the springs of action, the key to the workings of the man's mind. The results surprised him. The things that remained most clearly in his memory, he found, were not Connor's actions, or his considered statements of purpose, but certain little asides—remarks that he'd thrown off almost casually. . . .

"You're a man of peace, Maguire—that's why you don't count."

"It's the short run I'm interested in—and in the short run there's hope for the strong."

"When those who normally give orders cannot do so, the people will always look for orders elsewhere."

"All they needed was a first-class leader to inspire them. . . . I filled the need."

"You almost got the better of me—and that's something I'm not used to."

"You see, I am graduating the penalties. . . ."

As though he were God!

That hadn't been the language of a visionary, a romantic patriot, a man whose sacred cause came before everything—even himself. It had been the language, rather, of a cynical megalomaniac.

Was it possible, Maguire wondered, that Connor was no dedicated patriot after all, but a mere exploiter of the sentiment? A man who was deliberately using the ideals and aspirations of others for his own ends? That would explain why he had never taken the trouble to learn Irish properly, why he had known so little of the Tara legends until they were necessary to him, why he had scarcely heard of Ogham. He might have no interest in such things. . . . That would explain, too, his apparent contempt for his fellow-countrymen.

Perhaps he wasn't, after all, the complex character that he'd once seemed. Perhaps what Maguire had taken for complexity was mere duplicity. Connor had talked like a dreamer and behaved like a gangster—and that had been confusing. But he might be as simple in his aims as a man could be. Suppose he was just hungry for power, another would-be dictator? His area of operation was small, but he could still be in the same line of descent as the great dictators, the world-destroyers. His appetite could be the same. The appetite to rule and dominate, to see men cringe before him. . . . The primitive urge. . . . What was it he'd said, in that sardonic way of his—"Do you want to draw the teeth of Nature?" Perhaps it was king of the jungle he wanted to be, not leader of a free, united Ireland. He'd certainly struck Boland down with the ferocity of a jungle beast. . . .

Maguire's reflections didn't stop there. If he'd been mistaken in his first view of Connor, could he perhaps be wrong about Connor's prospects, too? Until now, the planned rising had seemed like the irrational, hopeless venture of a romantic Zealot—a venture that was bound to collapse when the crunch came. The pages of history were littered with such starry-eyed failures. But a rising planned and led by a cynical realist, a man not governed by emotion, a man of ruthless personal ambition, was another matter entirely. The new Connor was an infinitely more formidable figure than the old.

Could he succeed?

Once Maguire started to consider the question again, with detachment, his earlier optimism quickly-faded.

Connor would have everything in his favour on the night. There would be an atmosphere of holiday in Dublin. No one would be thinking of trouble. Connor's force, in its acceptable disguise, would achieve complete surprise. The police would be fully stretched, dealing with the crowds—and the drunks. Probably a large part of the army garrison would be given leave for the Pageant. Many of the key points would fall to Connor without a blow—unguarded places like the radio station and the Post Office. His commandos of well-armed men, attacking without warning or regard for life, might well capture the main arsenals before the regulars on duty could reach for their guns. Military airfields might be taken before a plane could fly, if he had the outlying forces that he claimed. And once the heavier weapons had fallen into his hands, there would be nothing in the country capable of stopping him. It was only too true that when he'd rounded up the Government leaders and the senior police and service officers, there'd be no one but himself to give orders. By its very daring, its sheer breath-taking magnitude, the plan could well succeed.

In forty-eight hours from now, Connor might be the master of Ireland!

It was a possibility that Maguire recoiled from with almost physical revulsion. Though he had never, like O'Rourke, had to fight for the freedom of his country, he deeply cherished the inheritance that other men had won. The prospect of arbitrary power in the hands of a callous adventurer was more than he could bring himself to contemplate. Failure by the old Connor would have been bad enough; success by the new one was unthinkable. Maguire saw his responsibility more starkly than ever.

Yet what could he do? He was now, almost literally, a man in chains. The new arrangements that Connor had made had taken the last scrap of privacy away from him. He was no longer allowed to work, or rest, or eat, or even sleep, behind closed doors. Always there was a guard at his elbow. Wherever he moved around the house, someone was watching. He was no longer permitted to stroll alone in the drive. If his presence was required out on the site, Connor accompanied him. If anyone called to see him, Connor was there to join in. . . . It was true that he could still denounce the plot openly in public—but then Nora and the boys would be killed. After the brutal act of terror against Boland, Maguire couldn't doubt it. . . . And no man could be expected to make such a sacrifice. He would give anything to thwart Connor's plans—anything but his wife and children. . . .

With feelings close to despair, Maguire turned to the chore on his desk. He had never felt less like penning a welcome to anyone—but he knew he must get it done. In an hour, Connor would be back. . . . Wearily, he ran his eye over the text that the Committee had approved. It read:

"The Committee of the Pageant of Tara warmly welcomes visitors to this historic site. Two thousand years ago it was the seat of the High Kings of Ireland. Legend gives us a picture of the life and customs of those times, but the truth lies hidden in the green mounds you see around you. It is the purpose of this Pageant to raise money for the excavation of the whole of Tara Hill. Splendid finds have already been made, but far more remain to be made. The Committee asks you to be generous on this great day."

It took Maguire only a few moments to translate the message into Irish for the first of the Welcome Board's three panels. Below, he wrote it out again in English for the second. Then, with the help of a book from his shelves, he transcribed the Irish much more laboriously into Ogham for the third panel. The lack of certain letters in the Ogham alphabet made it necessary to alter the wording of the text slightly, though not the sense.

Having transliterated the message, Maguire began to prepare the short, informative note about Ogham that was to go at the bottom of the Board. He quickly jotted down the main points—Ogham not a language but a form of writing ... oldest known form of Old Irish ... used mainly for inscriptions on memorial stones. ... Actual examples to be seen at foot of Board ... stones also found in western England, Wales, Isle of Man. ... He was running his eye down the descriptive material in the book to see if there was anything else of special interest when his attention was held by a sentence: "Formation of the letters by means of strokes ranging in number from 1 to 5 suggests that the signs may have been invented for use as a 'manual alphabet,' the five fingers held in different positions having been used to denote the letters in much the same way as the modern 'deaf-and-dumb' alphabet is used to-day."

A sign language ... !

In a moment, Maguire's apathy had vanished. Now that was an idea ... !

Was there, perhaps, some way he could use Ogham as a sign language himself—to convey information silently and secretly under Connor's very nose ?

Secretly. ... That was the important thing. That was what made the idea so attractive. If information about the rising could be passed to the authorities in absolute secrecy, Connor wouldn't know *how* they had found out. The very closeness of the guard under which Maguire was being held would make it appear impossible that he could have had a hand in it. He would have to be exonerated—suspicion would turn elsewhere. And there would be no reprisals against the family.

Maguire sat back, thinking about the mechanics of it. There was only one man with the knowledge to receive such a message—Seamus O'Rourke. A meeting could no doubt be arranged—with Connor sitting in, of course. Maguire could easily think of something he wanted to consult O'Rourke about in connection with the final arrangements for the Pageant. They could probably fix something for that afternoon. But then what . . . ? Maguire tried to imagine the circumstances. The last thing O'Rourke would be expecting would be a secret message in camouflaged Ogham signs. If he saw Maguire's fingers moving during conversation in an unaccustomed way, he would put it down to nervous strain rather than to Ogham. It would be the watchful Connor who would be more likely to suspect an attempt at communication. . . . Of course, there were other ways in which the symbols might be formed, besides the movement of fingers. Simpler and safer ways. Suppose they were sitting at a table. . . . Matches could be used. Five matches, arranged with apparent casualness against a line on the table top, the way one doodled on paper. As a pipe smoker, Maguire could quickly accumulate five spent matches on the table, and then fiddle with them as he talked. But again, would O'Rourke tumble to it, unless his attention had first been called in some way to what was going on? And could Maguire master the symbols in time? And what about the symbols that couldn't be represented by straight lines? And how long would it take to convey all the information that O'Rourke would need—letter by letter? It would take hours, if it were to be done nonchalantly, safely. . . . No—it simply wasn't feasible.

Maguire sighed. For a moment it had seemed such a promising idea. He still felt reluctant to abandon it altogether. . . . Was there any chance, he wondered, that he could somehow smuggle a *written* message in Ogham to O'Rourke, without danger of discovery . . . ?

He couldn't see how. The few letters he was allowed to write were closely scrutinised. The guards, treating him as an enemy since the execution of Boland, would let nothing go through that they didn't understand, And he certainly couldn't attempt to *pass* anything secretly to O'Rourke, with Connor's eyes upon him. ... No, a written message was even more impossible. ... Yet Ogham lent itself so perfectly to use as a code, Surely there was *some* way...

As Maguire gazed down at the sheet of paper before him, a far bolder plan suggested itself. Suppose, for the message of welcome he'd written in Ogham on that sheet, he substituted a secret message of his own—and then asked that it should be submitted to O'Rourke, the expert, to make sure there were no mistakes ... ?

No—that would be inviting disaster. Connor knew that Maguire had a book to refer to. He knew that Maguire was quite competent to do the job. He would suspect at once that an attempt was being made to pass a message. The only safe plan would be one that by its very nature aroused no suspicion at all. ...

It was then that Maguire suddenly had a quite fantastic idea.

Suppose he put his message on the Board of Welcome itself!

Chapter Fifteen

For a moment he sat aghast at the sheer audacity of the notion. It was, he told himself, an utterly insane idea. It would be incredibly dangerous. It probably wouldn't work. . . .

Then, as he thought a little more about it, he wondered. . . .

O'Rourke would certainly go and look at the Board on the morning of the Pageant. Though for the first hour or so he'd be with the rest of the Committee welcoming the Vice-President at Maguire's house and attending the opening ceremony, he'd be sure to make another round of the exhibits afterwards—and the Board would be a special attraction for him, because of his interest in Ogham and because he hadn't had a chance to see it yet. The probability was very great that he'd mentally decipher at least a word or two of the Ogham inscription—he'd be intrigued to see how Maguire had transliterated the message and anyway, with the alphabet in his head, it would be practically automatic. If the first words were something he didn't expect to be there, something startling—his own name, for instance—he'd read on to the end. . . . And he was a man who could be relied on to keep cool, to act with caution. After all, he was an old conspirator himself. He'd go off quietly and make contact with the highest authorities. What was more, he'd be listened to. . . .

Would Connor think of checking the Ogham writing before it went up? Maguire felt it was most unlikely. It wasn't as though the Board of Welcome was something he had suddenly thought up himself—it had been Connor's own idea. And it was Connor who had suggested that Maguire should make the transcription, who had had to bully him that morning into starting. Also, the very impudence of the plan would be a safeguard. Connor might well be looking out for some last-minute trick on Maguire's part, but he would hardly think that the effort would take the form of a brazen announcement on a public board.

Would anyone else decipher the message? Maguire decided that there was almost no chance of that. He knew of no one, apart from O'Rourke, who would be likely to have the Ogham letters in his head. Seamus himself had thought he was the only man in Ireland who had. There were other scholars who were interested in the subject and who would doubtless be at the Pageant, but they'd have no reason to question the accuracy of the Ogham translation and they'd soon pass on to other things. The chances of a premature, panicky exposure of the plot by some visitor were so slight as to be virtually non-existent.

In any case, Maguire thought that outside chance could be guarded against in the message. In a tentative way, he began to consider a possible form of words. He'd have to give the essential facts—and a warning. He took up a pencil—and put it down again. What he had in mind wasn't the sort of thing he could safely commit to paper in plain language. He sat back, and mentally rehearsed what he might say. . . .

"Seamus O'Rourke this is from Maguire. Connor intends to seize Dublin after march to-night all those in procession will be his men machine guns and grenades will be hidden under cloaks his plans include capture of key points in city and arrest of leaders in early hours my family is held hostage in unknown place tell authorities everything but impress on them source of knowledge must be kept secret or family may be killed if anyone else reads this say nothing here but carry out instructions exactly Maguire."

Yes, that would be the kind of thing. . . . Maguire wondered how it would compare in length with the official message, how it would look in the finished page. He put aside the sheet of paper he had already prepared for the signwriter and took another and began again. First he wrote out the Irish and English texts as before and then below them he set out his secret message in Ogham. This time he used the English language as the basis for his transliteration, since it was terser and would take less space. Once again he had to alter some of the words as he went along because of the gaps in the Ogham alphabet. Otherwise there were no difficulties.

Having completed the message, he added the note on the Ogham script at the bottom of the new version, as he had on the old one, and compared the two sheets. In each case, the Ogham was about the same length. To the casual eye, there was nothing whatever to choose between the versions. ... All he had to do now, he told himself grimly, was to destroy the first sheet and give the new one to Connor when he came ... But dare he ?

For the second time in a few days, Maguire tried to calculate the dangers of a course of action, to take all the possibilities into consideration.

Suppose Connor discovered the trick before it had a chance to succeed? Suppose he *did* check the Ogham at some stage? Well—then he'd probably do as he'd threatened and deprive the family of food and drink till the Pageant was over—as a lesson. Maguire would be powerless to prevent it, since withdrawal of co-operation would only lead to harsher sanctions. ... It was a pretty unpleasant thought—but was the risk and the prospect grave enough to rule out action absolutely? Maguire didn't think so.

Suppose the plan worked and the message got through to the authorities? Then Connor and his men would be rounded up. If the round-up was efficient, they would all be jailed. If it was inefficient, some might escape. Connor wasn't the type to surrender easily. Probably he would try to shoot his way out—and he might succeed.

In either event, though, he would have no further interest in the hostages—provided he didn't believe that Maguire had had a hand in the betrayal. If he was in prison, he would disclose their whereabouts, if only to make things easier for himself. If he was free, he would send orders to his guards to release them. He would have no reason not to.

The one terrifying hazard was that Connor would remain free and that in some way he *would* manage to connect Maguire with the disclosure of the plot. Then, on past form, he would take a bloody vengeance. . . . Yet Maguire couldn't imagine what evidence there could be, if the authorities were careful. The Board of Welcome could be dismantled immediately after the Pageant. Maguire himself could see that it was destroyed. The evidence would be gone. And all appearances would be on his side. . . .

Still, there *was* a risk. Maguire couldn't blind himself to that. The plan might even be called rash. But things had changed so much since he'd given his promise to Nora. The stakes were so much higher—on both sides. There was now the actual physical safety of the family at risk. Against that, there was not merely the certain loss of many lives, and untold suffering, but the possible triumph of an unprincipled dictator. . . .

Maguire gazed wretchedly at the two sheets of paper before him. He had to decide on one of them—but which? How *could* he take the chance . . . ? Yet how could he *not* take it . . . ?

He was still debating when Connor came in. Maguire had been so deep in his problem that he hadn't heard anything, he wasn't prepared. Before he had time to conceal the paper with the secret message on it, Connor was looking over his shoulder.

"Oh, you've finished it," he said. "Good—the signwriter's ready to start. . . ." He fingered the sheet that was dynamite. "Why two versions?"

For the fraction of a second, Maguire could think of no reply. Beads of sweat sprang out on his forehead. He couldn't say that one was a fair copy of the other—the versions had obviously been drawn with equal care. . . . Besides, with both sheets before him, Connor might spot the difference. . . . Then, just in time, the answer came to him.

"In this one," he said, "the Ogham is transliterated from the English, in the other one from the Irish. I wasn't sure which would be better."

"Oh, I'd use the one from the Irish," Connor said with a faint grin. "Much more suitable for a great national occasion . . . !" He continued to study the sheets. "You don't think we ought to include the Ogham alphabet at the bottom?"

Maguire hesitated. He knew he had only to say "maybe we ought" and that would be the end of his dilemma. The temptation was great. The words hovered on his lips—but he couldn't speak them.

He said, "Well, there's so much to go on the Board already that I doubt if there'll be room. Not that I care—but it would look a bit cramped. . . ."

Connor picked up the book Maguire had been using, glanced at the alphabet—and put the book down again. "I dare say you're right. . . . Then I'll get the man on to the painting right away. . . ." He held out his hand for the paper.

For a moment, Maguire's mind seemed to stand still. This was it! He couldn't pretend the versions weren't finished—he couldn't stall. He had to choose. The first version—and his chance would have gone for ever. The second—and anything could happen. The moment of decision—the decision that, once made, could never be retracted.

With a face like granite, Maguire picked up the sheet with the message to O'Rourke on it, and handed it to Connor. "That's the Irish one," he said.

Connor nodded. "You won't forget I'll be calling for you at four o'clock for the dress rehearsal in the Banqueting Hall. . . ." He put the paper in his pocket, and went out.

Chapter Sixteen

The next thirty-six hours were the most nerve-racking, the longest, and yet the busiest that Maguire had ever lived through. His greatest desire now was to shut himself away, to go into retreat till the outcome of his action was known. But Connor and the spurious Pageant preparations claimed him. There was no getting out of the dress rehearsal that afternoon, a prolonged and complex affair that he was supposed to be directing. It proved a fearful ordeal. Sorting out the confusion of men that swarmed in every sort of costume around the tents and the Banqueting Hall, getting them into their right places, making sure they all knew what was required of them, was not a thing he could do easily with half his mind. Yet half was taken up with the need to maintain the right public face, the right attitude. It was now more important than ever that he should seem to Connor not genuinely interested in anything but not visibly obstructive; that no trace of latent excitement or expectation should show in his manner. It was important, too, that without seeming to co-operate willingly with his guards he should remain under their eye for every second. Whereas a little earlier he would have welcomed the briefest opportunity to evade them, to stroll a dozen yards alone, to retire for a while behind closed doors, now he must give Connor no chance to say in retrospect, "That was the moment when he might have done it." Constant surveillance had become a condition of safety.

The strain was unrelieved—and the following day, the one before the Pageant, brought no respite. A final Committee meeting occupied the whole of the morning—a meeting of major importance where all the loose ends of the preparations had to be neatly tied up, and where the utmost concentration was required from the chairman. The session was resumed in the afternoon, and by five o'clock Maguire was close to mental exhaustion.

He could have rested for a while then—but there was something he still had to do for his own reassurance. He had heard Connor report at the meeting that the painting of the Board of Welcome would be finished that afternoon and that it would be erected just inside the entrance in the early evening. He had been careful to show no further interest in it since he'd handed the paper to Connor, but he was anxious now to see what the signwriter had made of the message, if he could do it in a natural way.

He had his chance around seven, when Connor suggested a perambulation of the site and a final check on everything. They started with the Banqueting Hall, and moved on from there. There had been a hectic rush to get other things finished besides the Welcome Board, but to Maguire the preparations looked as complete now as they were ever likely to be. The buildings had all been given their last touches, the refreshment booths were stocked, the museum treasures were in place and under police guard, the horses were assembled with their grooms in the near-by paddock, the kiosks were full of literature, the covered stalls in the market were groaning with goods. The great stream of deliveries which had cluttered the Navan road for days had become a mere trickle. Order had emerged from chaos, as Connor had said it would. The newspaper-men who had come out that evening for a preview and photographs had been understandably impressed. Everything was set—even, according to the forecast, the weather.

The Board of Welcome, with its Ogham stones around it, was the last thing they came to on their tour of inspection. The green, white and orange panels had been inscribed in black paint and looked very smart. The three texts, Maguire was relieved to see, had left only just enough room for the note on Ogham at the bottom—so there was no possibility that Connor would change his mind about the alphabet. The Ogham text had been copied as Maguire had been careful to write it on the paper, with no gaps between words, so there was no reason why anyone should doubt that it was an exact transliteration of the words above. Even to Maguire, who knew its deadly content, it *looked* safe.

The signwriter—not one of Connor's own men—was still there, waiting for the last lorry to take him home to Dublin.

"Maybe you'd like to check over that Ogham, Mr. Maguire," he said, "now that you're here. . . . I believe it's all right—but it wasn't the easiest kind of work. . . ." He produced the original paper, now very grubby, and gave it to Maguire.

"You've made a nice job of it," Maguire said. His required indifference to the project as a whole needn't, he thought, exclude personal praise for the man. He opened the paper and stood back and began to go over the Ogham text, letter by letter, comparing it with what was on the Board. He couldn't see whether Connor was looking at him or not. He felt exposed, vulnerable—but he knew he must keep quite cool. He mustn't be too quick, or too slow. Just natural. God, how hard it was to be natural! With careful deliberation, he completed his inspection. "Yes," he said, "there's not a single mistake. Well done!" He squeezed the paper into a ball and tossed it into a litter basket. He hadn't thought of it before, but that scrap of paper could have been fatal evidence against him. It was all right now, though . . . Connor was nodding to the man, and beginning to move away with Maguire.

"I think that Board was rather a good idea of mine," Connor said. "It definitely adds tone to the Pageant."

Maguire looked at him uncomprehendingly. "I can't imagine why you should care. . . . The Pageant means no more to you than to me."

"On the contrary," Connor said, "it means a great deal to me. The more genuine it looks, the safer I shall be. It's only because I've seemed really interested in it that I've been able to build up such trust everywhere. . . . In any case," he added, with a grin, "the new Ireland will certainly want to have Tara excavated. I hope we make a big profit."

Maguire was silent for a moment. Then he said, "I still think you'll fail."

"We can't fail. We've thought of everything." Connor took a

folded paper from his pocket and opened it out. "Perhaps you'd like to see our Proclamation."

Maguire glanced through it with an expressionless face. It was a rousing call to the people to support the rebellion, which would bring freedom and a united Ireland. Its stirring tone and content reminded Maguire of the famous Proclamation that had gone up at the time of the Easter Rising. This one had everything that the earlier one had had—everything, Maguire thought, except sincerity.

"It's fortunate that one of my men happens to be a printer," Connor said. "He's been working hard—mostly at night. By next Sunday morning these will be all over Dublin—and a dozen other towns."

"I suppose it hasn't occurred to you," Maguire said, "that one of your hundreds of men might be unreliable. That one of them might even have been planted on you by the police. Such things have happened."

Connor smiled. "I'm afraid it's no good your clinging to that hope, Maguire. I know all the men personally—and I can trust them all."

"As you trusted Boland?"

"He was weeded out in time. There will be no second Boland."

Maguire shrugged. "Well, I can tell you this—in your place I wouldn't feel so confident. . . . I hope you won't hold *me* responsible if anything goes wrong, that's all. Considering how I've resisted temptation, I'd hate my family to suffer for a betrayal by someone else".

Connor said, "You just go on resisting temptation, Maguire, and you'll be all right."

In his room that night, Maguire's hopes rose steadily. The first of the hazards had been safely negotiated. Connor clearly had had no suspicions about the Welcome Board—and now that it was erected he was unlikely to give it another thought. To-morrow, the way would be open for O'Rourke.

Now that he'd seen the Board himself, Maguire felt more confident than ever that O'Rourke would read the message. To anyone knowing the Ogham alphabet as Seamus did, those first few letters would stand out like a beacon. And the old man would be discreet. He would not only watch his own step—he would do everything to ensure that the source of the information wasn't disclosed. He would probably go straight to the Prime Minister—that was what Maguire would have done in his place. And then fade out of the picture, so that no one could connect him with what followed. . . . Only a handful of people would need to be told all the facts, and they'd be highly placed and responsible. There'd be virtually no chance of a leakage.

Maguire wondered when and where the authorities would strike. It would probably be almost noon before the information reached them—and then it would take time to mobilise the necessary force. The late afternoon, perhaps . . . ? They might try to round up Connor's men while they were in the Banqueting Hall—while they were still unarmed, except for a few revolvers. . . . Or would such an operation seem too dangerous, with the public milling around in thousands . . . ? Maybe they'd wait till the evening, when the rebels were preparing in their tents? To leave it later than that would be to invite a major armed clash on the road to Dublin—or worse, in the city itself.

It wasn't going to be an easy task, Maguire could see. Time would be very short. But at least it would be the regular forces now who had surprise on their side—not Connor. They could pick the place and the moment. They'd know precisely the strength they had to deal with, too. . . . Anyhow, they were the experts—it would be up to them to find a way. Maguire felt sure that they would. In thirty-six hours from now, he told himself, the rising might be crushed—and he and Nora and the boys might be reunited.

On that note of hope and trust, he finally dozed off.

The morning of the Pageant was as fine as the forecast had promised. Almost before the day had broken the site was astir, and from then on activity mounted rapidly. Traffic on the road from Dublin soon began to build up as people poured out of the city—first, police in great numbers to control the route and the crowds; then those who were going to take charge of the turnstiles, the racing, the exhibits, the buffets and the rest; then the great, exuberant mass of the public. ... The coach parties, waving tricolours from open windows and already full of the carnival spirit; the innumerable private cars, packed to capacity with children and prams and picnic gear; the traps and gigs and jalopies and farm-carts, their horses gay with rosettes and ribbons; the pedal cyclists, heads down in massed formation; and, from all the neighbouring villages, the pedestrians. Wherever there was a road or a lane that could end at the Hill, there was a lively, chattering column happily making its way. Long before the time of the Pageant's official opening, several thousands of visitors were already dispersed around the site. Many of them had come in fancy costumes of their own making—hardly authentic period pieces, but unquestionably colourful. An air of gaiety and high expectation was blowing pleasantly through Tara.

Maguire was more expectant than anyone. Expectant—and by now unbearably excited. There had been no hitch in his plan, and he didn't foresee any. Connor was wholly preoccupied with his official and unofficial duties. It was just a question of waiting—and keeping rising hopes well hidden. ...

At nine-thirty the Committee members began to assemble at the house, as Maguire had asked them to. The trade union man arrived first, then Mrs. O'Flaherty, bright and loquacious, then the stockbroker and Liam Driscoll together. Soon the room was filled with chatter—about the Pageant, about the masses of people who were pouring in, about when the Vice-President would arrive, about the great day it was going to be, and what a pity it was that Nora Maguire was missing it all. Maguire, aware all the time of Connor's watchful eye, made a visible effort to seem in high spirits with the others, while losing no opportunity to lapse into sullen silence on his own. This was no moment to seem genuinely cheerful. ...

He was doing, he thought, fairly well, when at nine forty-five he was called into the hall to speak on the telephone. Connor, excusing himself from the company, went with him. The guard at the table—now ostensibly a Pageant *aide*—handed the receiver to Maguire. "It's Mr. O'Rourke," he said.

Maguire took the phone, frowning. "Hullo, Seamus. . . . Why aren't you on your way?"

"Och, I'm the most disappointed man in Dublin," O'Rourke said. "I slipped on the stairs when I was coming down to the car just now, and though I doubt if it's anything serious I've a bruise on my leg as big as a saucer and I can't walk a step."

"*No.* . . ."

"It's a fact. . . . And it had to happen to-day, of all days!"

"Couldn't you get someone to lift you into the car?" Maguire struggled to keep the desperation out of his voice. "If you could drive out here, at least you could take a look at the Hill from the road. It's a fine sight, Seamus."

"I'm sure it is, but I'm not. up to it, and that's the truth. I'm as sore as if I'd been dropped from a height. . . . Will you tell the Committee what's happened, and offer my apologies?"

"I will, of course," Maguire said. "I'm terribly sorry, Seamus—and the Committee will be, too. We'll miss you. . . . I hope you'll soon be all right again—I'll come and see you when I can. . . . Goodbye." He hung up.

Connor said, "What's wrong with the old man?"

"He's had a fall," Maguire told him. "He won't be coming. . . ."

"Too bad," Connor said.

Maguire nodded, and went into the sitting-room to tell the Committee. He could scarcely believe his bad luck. He no longer had to make any effort to look depressed when Connor's eyes were on him. He felt crushed, beaten. The duel was over—and Connor had won.

127

Chapter Seventeen

The Pageant, all agreed, was a fantastic success. In any other circumstances, Maguire would have taken the greatest pride and pleasure in it.

The Banqueting Hall, as had been intended, was the chief attraction. The building itself, with its elaborate thatch, its skilfully woven withies, its carved and decorated posts, was a work of art, and the scene within was as splendid and glittering as any of the ancient descriptions. First, there was Cormac, flaxen-haired and bearded, looking every inch a king in his white tunic, his crimson cloak fastened with a magnificent brooch, his golden belt and torque, his gold-network shoes with their golden buckles. Even his gestures were regal, as he clapped his hands in traditional welcome of a new guest or beat authoritatively for silence on the silver gong in front of him. Then came the warriors, scarcely less magnificently attired, gnawing their prescribed hunks of meat, tossing the bones to scavenging dogs, taking long draughts of ale from drinking horns, slapping each other on the back with deep-throated laughter, pretending sudden quarrels—a fierce and formidable band, who looked as though they might be off on a cattle raid at any moment. Farther down the hall came the groups of craftsmen, each group occupying a separate, box-like compartment with rushes on the floor and furs and rugs over the rushes, and each with its professional insignia hung aloft. Three fires blazed in a centre aisle, with cooks beside them tending roasting carcasses on spits. At a great vat of ale, cup-bearers constantly replenished the horns. Nine harpers in grey mantles, with crystal rings on their arms and silver torques round their throats, made traditional music with their small Irish harps. Fools cavorted, poets recited barbaric tales, druids busied themselves with strange ceremonies. Both inside and outside the Hall there was incessant noise, shouting and laughter and a huge, earthy enjoyment. The benches alongside the Hall were packed to capacity, and all day long visitors filed by to see the spectacle, some of them many times.

Elsewhere on the crowded hill, the scene was hardly less lively and colourful. Everyone was finding plenty to interest them. The foreign tourists, festooned with cameras and weighed down with guide-books and literature, seemed particularly drawn to the more sedate exhibits—the reconstructed village and the beehive hut, the Museum with its wealth of ancient Irish treasures, and the actual mounds of Tara Kill that were the reason for everything. The Board of Welcome, with its fringe of Ogham stones, was fully justifying itself as an attraction. Most people stopped to read the words on the Board, and there were many comments on the Ogham, some interested, some ribald. No one showed any sign of knowing the alphabet. Maguire had been only too right about that.

The less serious attractions had an even wider appeal. The horse-racing was soon in full swing, and the "tote" coining money for the Committee. A game of hurley had been started, and wrestling bouts organised. Jugglers and fortune-tellers were doing good business, and the stalls in the market were being well-patronised. Groups of people were engaged in folk dancing and chorus-singing. There was music of a kind on every hand—from bone men and fiddlers and tube-players, from flutes and Irish pipes. Buffoons in painted masks amused the crowd with harmless practical jokes. Everyone was having a wonderful time.

As the afternoon slipped by, the nature of the Pageant changed. By now, everything had been seen, and the huge, excited crowd was in the mood for its own festivities. The day soon took on the character of a gigantic celebration in which everyone joined. People began dancing among themselves, first to pipes and drums and then to the more sophisticated bands that the Committee had engaged. Merriment and laughter filled the air—and empty bottles covered the ground. It was clear that the revelry would go on for many hours yet.

Maguire, after the opening ceremony and the first official round of the exhibits, had seen little of the Pageant. Connor, as the time drew on and the crowd grew thicker, had decided that the task of escorting him everywhere was too onerous, and once it was clear that his absence from the site wouldn't be noticed, had confined him to the house again under guard. Maguire was thankful to be out of it all. O'Rourke's telephone call had been a bludgeoning shock and he still felt dazed and sick. The gaiety and excitement outside were now a hideous back-cloth to the grim events ahead. The fact that he had gone to the extremity of risk to defeat Connor, that no man in his position could have done more, gave him no satisfaction. His mind was wholly occupied with thoughts of the guns and explosives in the tents, of the cold-blooded preparations for battle and slaughter.

The hours dragged by. He tried to distract himself with a book, telling himself he was a helpless onlooker now and must reconcile himself to the part. But the distant strains of the dance bands beat in his ears and he found concentration impossible. He got himself some food, shadowed at every step by one of the guards—but he couldn't eat it. He lit his pipe, usually so soothing, but it tasted bitter and he had to abandon it. He paced restlessly about the room, going constantly, to the window. Only an hour or so to dusk. . . . Soon, the procession would be starting. He'd be kept here under guard all night, he supposed. . . .

It wasn't until darkness began to fall that anything happened. Then there was the sound of voices outside, a step in the hall—and Connor came in. For a moment, Maguire didn't recognise him. He was wearing a dark wig and beard, a tunic and a flowing cloak. He had dressed himself as a warrior, like the others—and a warrior fully accoutred. As the folds of his cloak swung against his side, Maguire was able to make out the hard line of a weapon.

Connor's manner was brusque. "You're coming with us, Maguire," he said. From under the cloak he produced a bundle—another cloak, a tunic and a belt. "They were meant for Boland—but he won't be needing them now! Get them on!"

Maguire picked up the tunic. "Why do I have to come? Do you need a witness to murder?"

"Your friends will be expecting you in Dublin—I wouldn't want you to be missed from the finale. . . . Anyway, I'll feel happier if you're under my eye."

"I'm a poor hand with a horse," Maguire said.

"You'd need to be, to have any difficulty with the ones I've seen. . . . Hurry up, it's time we left."

In silence, Maguire put on the tunic and the belt, and draped the cloak around him.

The two guards left the house with Connor and Maguire, their watching duties over. In the semi-darkness, the little party skirted the side of the Hill and made their way to the paddock. The field was packed with Cormac's warriors—faceless men, anonymous under their beards and cloaks. Each had his horse beside him, saddled or just caparisoned. Some had already mounted. The horses were neighing, snorting, snuffling and stamping. Flares had been lit and raised on staves and spears, casting a lurid glow over the scene. Everything was set for departure. Connor, gripping Maguire's arm, led him through the throng to where Cormac was waiting, with two spare hacks. The one Maguire was given was a quiet mare, who took no objection to him. Connor had a black horse, a livelier one, but he controlled it with ease.

"All right," Connor called to Cormac, "let's go."

A trumpet sounded, and the cavalcade moved slowly off towards the field gate and the road. The paddock had been for some time the chief centre of interest and a huge crowd jostled against the police cordon, waving and cheering as the column passed. Cormac was at its head, as fine a figure mounted as on foot. Immediately behind him rode Connor and Maguire, side by side, with Donnelly and Regan following. Behind them, in no special order, came the main body of the soldiers. As the procession reached the road and turned towards Dublin, someone began to sing Moore's haunting song —"the harp that once through Tara's halls the soul of music shed...."—and the whole of the great phalanx took up the words.

Connor glanced across at Maguire, his face more sardonic than ever in the torchlight. "It's a tribute to you," he said. "The man who made it all possible!"

Chapter Eighteen

As the cavalcade turned southwards along the main road the police cordon was raised and the sightseers who wanted to accompany it and cheer it on its way were allowed to fall in behind. There were cyclists by the score, and packs of running children and, at first, even some active walkers. Behind them came cars and coaches in a seemingly endless line, their headlamps floodlighting the procession. The enthusiasm of the crowd was more than matched by the warriors, who appeared to have nothing on their minds but the entertainment of the public. They sang stirringly for mile after mile, old ballads that everyone knew and national songs that had certainly been unknown to the real Cormac. Between the songs, trumpets sounded and harps were strummed. There was some brandishing of silver-painted wooden swords, as well as of the flaring torches; pretences of drinking from horns; bawdy exchanges with people on the roadside; a convincing air of swashbuckling bonhomie. The last act of the day's entertainment had been as well thought out as everything that had gone before, and the crowd loved it.

Ahead, the road had been cleared of vehicles by the police, and the horsemen passed without obstruction between lines of waving, cheering sightseers. In every village on the route, the windows. and the doorways were packed with people; in every village street, boys with official rosettes were busy rattling collecting boxes. As the miles fell away behind, some of the folk who had set out from Tara gave up the pursuit, but each village contributed a fresh quota of followers. By the time the column neared the half-way mark, the roadside was beginning to be lined even where there were no houses. Quite a lot of people, evidently, had come out from Dublin for the evening. The collecting boxes filled rapidly.

Maguire, riding beside the silent, preoccupied Connor, felt chilled by the masquerade. The horror of what lay ahead weighed more heavily on him with every beat of the hooves under him. He had never been more reluctant to accept the inevitable than he was now that the drama was actually unfolding. It seemed incredible that with all the knowledge he had he should be so powerless. He tried to work out what might happen when they reached Dublin, seeking some loophole, clutching at the hope of an eleventh-hour miracle. The procession, he knew, was to reach its formal end by Nelson's Pillar in O'Connell Street. After that, the force would no doubt begin to split up into the operational bands that Connor had planned. They would hang around for an hour or two, waiting for the crowds to go home and the streets to clear. Then, as though going home themselves, they would move towards their objectives, unquestioned, unimpeded. Would they take him along too? Maguire doubted it. They'd be more likely to leave him somewhere under guard. They'd be too afraid he might throw caution away in the heat of the moment and shout a desperate last-minute warning at the barrack gates. They'd never give him that chance. . . . In any case, he knew he wouldn't take it. It was pointless to think any more about what would happen. There was no way out.

Until now the cavalcade had been moving at little more than a fast walking speed, but Connor, glancing at his watch, presently cantered forward to Cormac with a quiet instruction, and at once the pace increased. Before long, all the footsloggers had dropped far behind. Ahead, the lights of Dublin were growing rapidly brighter in the sky. Only a few more miles to go! Very soon the procession reached the place where the horses were to be left, and the column, shepherded by grinning policemen, turned off into a field and dismounted. There was a period of some confusion as the animals were sorted out among their waiting owners and grooms—and a further short delay while the men refreshed themselves. Then the procession was off again at a steady marching pace, eight abreast across the road. The traffic behind, held up by the police during the interval, closed in once more.

The men were more subdued now. Some of them, Maguire saw, were having a little trouble with the guns under their cloaks. Riding had been easier. For the first time, there was a feeling of tension in the ranks. . . . Connor, sensing it, called to the men to sing again—and at once they responded. He might be a villain, Maguire thought, but he was certainly a leader. Cool, watchful, confident. . . .

The crowds had grown greater than ever. Ahead, both sides of the road were thickly lined—half Dublin must be out. . . . A signpost glimmered in the light of a torch. Four miles to go. Less than an hour. . . .

For fifteen minutes the column swung along at a fine pace. Then there was an unexpected check. A mounted police officer came trotting towards them between the cheering lines of onlookers, and reined beside Cormac. Connor, with raised hand, halted the procession. The officer had a harassed look.

"There's been a bit of a shindig down at the bridge," he said, thumbing over his shoulder. "I reckon you'd do better to go through the gate here and join the road farther down or you won't be in Dublin for hours."

"What's the trouble?" Connor asked.

"Och—too much of the liquor, and a gang of roughnecks on the rampage. "We've eight broken heads down there—it's been like the end of the world and the devil come for his own! And now the ambulance has got itself jammed against the bridge to make things worse. . . . If you like I'll lead the way through the field—it's not a great distance."

"Right, you do that," Connor said.

The officer opened the gate and rode through it, and on through another gate. The procession followed him, the men out of step now, feeling their way over the rough ground. It was suddenly very dark, for the following cars and bicycles with their lights had been halted by the police, and most of the flares the men were carrying had given out. The column stumbled on. They were descending a sloping bank, with converging hedges on either side. Over to the left, Maguire could see lights round the obstruction at the bridge. Someone was shouting in drunken argument. Evidently the shindig was still going on—but now they were beginning to draw away from it. The police officer turned and called encouragingly, "Another hundred yards and you'll be back on the road. . . ."

Then, without warning, it happened. Out of the darkness, a voice cried "Halt!"—a voice enormously amplified by a loud hailer. Taken by surprise, the column froze. "Sean Connor," the hailer blared, "this is the army. We know your intentions. We know you are carrying arms. You're outnumbered and encircled. Surrender, or you'll be shot down to a man."

In the same instant, three searchlights flashed on—one from ahead, one from the left, one from the right—drilling the column with hard white beams.

There was a moment of deathly silence. No one moved. Connor's face was like parchment in the glare of the light. He shot one incredulous, uncomprehending glance at Maguire. Then he turned and shouted at the top of his voice, "Scatter, lads!—we'll live to fight another day." A second later he was away, bent low, doubling back up the field with his cloak flying. The ranks began to break. The loud hailer barked an order. A fearful burst of fire shattered the night. All of it was directed at Connor. In a moment he fell riddled, and lay still,

Leaderless now, and hopelessly exposed, the men hesitated. New sounds broke the silence—the engines of armoured cars, closing in. Soldiers, steel-helmeted and equipped for battle, moved in behind them with sub machine-guns. The loud hailer crackled again. "Hands above your heads, if you want to live . . . !" Cormac's hands shot up, and Donnelly's, and Regan's, and all the others' followed—Maguire's, too. A soldier dragged his cloak off. Rough hands searched him for arms. He made no protest. This was clearly no time to try and identify himself, when all was menace and confusion. Around him, sten guns and grenades, revolvers and ammunition clips were being piled. Now the rebels were being marshalled into groups and led away. In a moment Maguire was being hustled along with about twenty other men, back to the road and into a waiting lorry. Guards climbed on to the tail-board and squatted there, pointing their guns, as the lorry roared away towards Dublin.

No one spoke on the journey. The men seemed stunned by the suddenness and magnitude of the disaster that had overtaken them. Jam-packed in the small, dark space, they stood and swayed together in sweating silence. Maguire, with someone's elbow in his back and an iron stanchion pressing against his shoulder, shared their discomfort of body—but not of mind. At least, not at first. Dazed shock was giving way to overwhelming relief and thankfulness. He had never really believed that there would be an informer in Connor's camp—but against all expectations there must have been. The miracle had happened. The rising was crushed, the ringleader was dead—it was all over. Nora and the children would be released. . . .

He stopped short there. Suddenly, sharply, he was back with his personal problem.

If Connor had lived, he would undoubtedly have given orders for the family to be set free. He would have known for certain that Maguire could have had nothing to do with the debacle. And his orders would have been obeyed. But Connor was dead—and no one else could give any orders. Only Connor and the two guards, Maguire remembered, had known where the hostages were. So everything depended on the guards—who might well blame Maguire for the collapse. And that wasn't all. . . .

Fear gripped Maguire again as he recalled what Connor had told him about the guards. Two ruthless men, specially picked for their toughness, both wanted for murder under other names. Men with nothing to lose by more killing. Men who would have only one thought—to do what was best for themselves, without pity. If they let the family go free, they would know that Nora would describe them, that they would have no chance of escape. If they silenced the hostages, they would be safe. . . .

Maguire could scarcely wait now for the lorry to reach its destination. A search must be started at once—a nation-wide search.

He couldn't imagine how it could be done, when so little was known—but there must be *some* way. A radio appeal to the public for information, an appeal and a warning to the guards, a message from Donnelly perhaps. . . . The police would have ideas. . . . The thing was to get them started—there wasn't a moment to lose. He must identify himself to the authorities straight away. . . . If he had been near enough to the tail-board he would have tried there and then to speak to the soldiers, to dissociate himself from the rebels, but he was deep in the interior, unable to move. . . . He waited, hardly knowing how to contain himself.

The minutes passed, seeming like hours. Then the lorry began to slow. Suddenly it turned sharply, and jerked to a halt. A rough voice shouted, "All out . . . !" The lorry began to empty. Maguire clambered down with the others. They were in a large, stone-flagged courtyard lit with searchlights and packed with police and soldiers and armoured cars. There was a lot of noise, an atmosphere of tension and near-violence. Maguire looked round for someone to speak to, someone in authority, but a policeman gave him a shove and in a moment he was being hustled off with the others. Desperately he addressed the soldier nearest to him as he stumbled on. "I've got to see an officer," he said. "I'm not one of the rebels—it's all a mistake. My name's Maguire—I'm . . ."

"Shut your gob!" the soldier said, and jabbed a gun-barrel into his back, pushing him forward. Before he could speak again he was being swept through an open door into a big, bare room crowded with prisoners and lined with guards.

As he entered, silence fell. Everyone in the room was staring at him. Among the many familiar faces, one stood out—the face of Waugh, the man who had seemed to hate him even when everything was going well.

"There he is—the bloody informer!" Waugh cried. "Let's get him!" There was a surge forward, Guards shouted, shots rang out. Someone struck Maguire a savage blow in the face, and he went down, Men were kicking him. Pain tore through his body—fearful pain. Then he knew nothing more.

Chapter Nineteen

A hundred miles away, and some nine hours later, the two men specially picked by Connor to take over the guarding of Nora and the children from MacEoin and Kiernan were crouching over a portable radio, waiting for the first news of the rising. Nora was standing by the window with her back to them, also waiting. The children were playing upstairs,

The atmosphere was tense. The guards, who had been sufficiently confident an hour ago to wonder whether Connor himself would come to the microphone to make the victory announcement, had fallen silent now, as though they had suddenly realised that their lives could depend on what they heard.

Nora herself was keyed up almost to breaking point. The strain of being forever watched, of living in squalid proximity with the two guards, of constant pretence and evasion with the children, and of uncertainty about what was happening at Tara, had become almost unbearable. Since the middle of the week she had had no news of James. She had been told of his fruitless visit to the empty cottage and the discovery of his intentions, but that was all. She didn't even know if any reprisals had been taken against him. All she knew for certain was that he had been unable to do anything more, anything effective, or she would have heard. So Connor's plan had presumably been carried out, and over everything—personal and national—a great question mark hung. She feared desperately what she might hear now—and she felt horribly alone.

She glanced at her watch. Only seconds to go. . . . Yes, here it came—the time signal. She stood in frozen rigidity.

"This is Radio Eireann," a man's voice said. "Here is the news. ... An attempt during the night to overthrow the Government of Eire by force has ended in total failure. The ringleader, a man named Sean Connor, has been killed, and the bulk of his supporters are now in prison. ...."

With a faint sigh, Nora turned. The guards weren't looking at her. They were gaping stupidly at each other, bewildered, incredulous. Nora pulled up a wooden box and sat down to listen to the rest.

The report covered familiar ground at first—Connor's use of the Pageant as a cloak for his activities, the concealment of arms, the gathering of forces, the procession. Then came an account of the army ambush, of Connor's death while trying to escape, and of the bloodless round-up. With the total collapse of the rising in Dublin, the announcer said, the rebels' plans to extend the revolt to provincial towns and garrisons had come to nothing. The whole of Eire was quiet and normal. ...

One of the guards got to his feet and began to stuff some things into a rucksack.

The report went on to give some background information about Connor. He was presented as an ambitious and unscrupulous adventurer who had succeeded in duping simpler souls. Fortunately, the Government had become aware of his activities in time. The plot had been given away, the announcer said, by a man whom Connor had relied on to aid the revolt in the West, but who had actually been an undercover member of the Security forces. ... Then the bulletin told of Maguire, the chairman of the Pageant Committee, who through an accidental discovery had been caught up in the web and forced into silence by the kidnapping of his family. Now that the plot had been foiled, and through no action of his, he confidently looked forward to the safe return of his wife and children. A description of Nora and the boys followed, and an appeal for the help of the public in tracing them. If any harm came to them, the men who were known to be guarding them would be punished with the utmost seventy of the law. ... At the end of the bulletin, the announcer said, the Prime Minister would be broadcasting to the nation. ...

The guard who was packing his rucksack said, "Turn the bloody thing off!" The second guard did so. Beads of sweat glistened under his red hairline. After a moment he started packing, too.

All the tension had gone out of Nora now. James was obviously safe, or they wouldn't have said he was looking forward to the return of his family. The rising was over—and they were all safe. There was nothing more to worry about. To Nora, too, it seemed like a miracle.

"Well—what now?" she asked.

"The quickest way out of auld Ireland for us," the first guard said. "Och—'tis a desperate thing. That decent man . . . ! Who would have thought it could happen?" He picked up the radio and took it out to the car.

Nora looked out of the window. The sun was just beginning to break through the morning mist that veiled the mountains. It was going to be a wonderful day.

Presently she went outside. The guards had finished gathering up their belongings and were climbing into the car. "We're away, Mrs. Maguire," one of them said. "It's sorry we are we can't take you with us, but you see for yourself how it is—we'll need a bit of a start. . . . You'll be all right, though, you won't be stuck. . . . Just walk down the hill till you come to the village, and say who you are, and there'll be plenty of folk who'll look after you. . . . Goodbye, now—and the best of luck to you."

As the engine started, the children came running out. One of the men waved to them. Then the car bounced away down the track, rounded a bend, and was gone.

For a moment, Nora felt curiously at a loss. It was strange to be free again, to be able to make decisions, to have to organise things for herself. . . . Then she realised that there was actually nothing to organise, There was no point in packing—they couldn't hope to carry their things down with them. They had had a good breakfast and wouldn't be hungry for hours. If they grew thirsty, there'd be water in the streams . . . All they had to do was leave.

"We're going home, children," she said.

141

Gavin looked at her in surprise. "Is the holiday over?"

"Yes—the holiday's over. We're going back to Daddy."

"Why has the car gone without us? Is it coming back?"

"No, darling, we'll have to walk. Those men have left us. . . . I'm afraid they weren't really very nice."

"*I* think they were nice," Rory said.

Nora smiled. "I'll just get my bag," she said, "and then we'll set off—exactly as we are. We'll get someone else to collect our things afterwards. It's a lovely morning for a walk—you'll enjoy it. . . ."

It was a long way to the valley, particularly for Rory—a full five miles of rough going on the stony track. But it was all downhill, and the air was crisp, and there were lots of new things to interest the children—a granite outcrop shaped like a man's face, a rushing waterfall, an abandoned cabin, and—farther down—thatched turf stacks and wonderful hedges of wild fuschia. Nora had a moment of slight concern when the track forked and she didn't know which way to go, but as they stood debating she caught the sound of church bells away to the right and that settled it.

When, towards the end of the hike, the boys began visibly to flag, she took their hands, one on each side of her, and said, "Would you like me to tell you now about the box you found in the tent?"

They brightened at once. "Oh, yes, please!" Gavin said eagerly.

So Nora told them the real story of their adventure—a careful, edited version, but with nothing essential left out. The boys drank it in avidly, their sore feet entirely forgotten. It was, as James had prophesied, the best cops-and-robbers story they'd ever heard—and one they'd actually been concerned in themselves! They were still asking excited questions when they reached the outskirts of the village—and a telephone box. Nora stopped.

"I'm going to ring Daddy and tell him we're coming," she said hopefully.

She still had no idea where they were—but the name of the exchange on the telephone, Dalbally, was vaguely familiar. She rather thought it was somewhere in County Tipperary. She gave the Tara number to the operator, asking for the charge to be transferred, and waited. But there was no reply.

"Daddy isn't there," she said, emerging. "Let's see if we can find a policeman."

There were a lot of people in the street as they walked on into the village. It was Sunday morning, and almost church time, but that wasn't the only reason. People were gathered in little groups, talking earnestly, solemnly. About the morning's sensational news, of course. A priest passed, with a "God bless!" and a curious glance at the trio. Nora hesitated—but decided a policeman would be better. It wasn't until they reached the wide square that Gavin spotted one. He was leaning on a bicycle, chatting with two other men.

Nora addressed him. "I'm Nora Maguire," she said, "the wife of James Maguire, and these are my children. We were kidnapped by the rebels. You must have heard about it on the radio."

The policeman gazed at them for a long moment. "Mother of God, I believe you are!"

"We are, I'm telling you. We've been up in the mountains. We have to get to Dublin."

The policeman nodded slowly, still staring. "Sure, and you have to get to Dublin," he said, "and it's meself that'll put you on your way." He looked at the two men. "In Dalbally!" he said. "Imagine!"

Chapter Twenty

Maguire had survived his beating. He returned to full consciousness a little after midday to find himself in bed in a hospital room. His head was bandaged and his chest was strapped and he was extremely sore all over, but as his muzziness passed and he remembered what had happened, he felt lucky to be alive. He had been rescued by the soldiers, the nurse told him, before any serious damage had been done—a fractured rib, a cut head, and some bruises, that was all. In a week or two he'd be as good as new.

He was about to ask her if there had been any word of the family when she forestalled him.

"Your wife is here, Mr. Maguire," she said.

"*Here . . . !*" For a moment it seemed too good to be true. Then he gave a long, relaxed sigh. "Oh—thank God!"

"She's been in and out several times, waiting for you to come round. . . . I'll tell her she can talk to you now."

"Please."

He lay and watched the door. In a few seconds he heard her step and she was at the bedside, pressing her face to the unbandaged side of his head. "Darling," she murmured. "Oh, darling. . . ."

"Nora!" Maguire held her as though he would never let her go again. "I can hardly believe it. . . . Are you all right? Are the children all right?"

"Yes, they're fine. . . . I've left them at Seamus's house—Caithlin's looking after them. . . . I tried to ring you at home, twice—when I got no reply I went straight to him. He's told me everything. He's coming along to see you soon. . . . Oh, darling, I know you must be feeling awful—but isn't it marvellous it's all over. . . ."

"It's marvellous that you're back. . . ." His hand tightened on hers. "Nora, I was so afraid for you. . . . Where were you? What happened?"

"You mean this morning . . . ? Nothing very much, really." She told him how she'd listened to the radio, and how the guards had left, and about the walk down the mountain, and how the policeman at Dalbally had found a car to take them to Dublin.

"Well, I never thought they'd go off just like that," Maguire said, as she finished. "I was afraid they might kill you—you knew so much about them. . . . I still don't know why they didn't. A couple of desperate characters, men who'd murdered already. . . ."

Nora looked at him in astonishment. "Whatever gave you that idea?"

"Connor told me. . . ."

"But, darling, they weren't like that at all. They were under Connor's spell, of course, and I dare say they'd have done most things if he'd told them to—but they weren't really tough. . . . And they couldn't have been kinder to us—especially Boland. . . ."

"*Boland . . . !*" Maguire stared at her.

"Yes—the man from Malin who took Rory's bear for you—you remember. He was one of the guards who took over when MacEoin and the other man left."

Maguire's face was stiff with incredulity. "But Boland was shot—I was going to tell you. Connor believed Boland had told me where the cottage was in return for the whisky, and shot him as a traitor. . . ."

"Darling, he couldn't have done. . . ."

"But, Nora, I heard the shot—I *saw* Boland being carried away on a stretcher. They were going to bury him. . . . It was definitely Boland, I saw his face."

For a moment, Nora looked as bewildered as Maguire himself. Then she said, "Well, I can assure you he's perfectly all right—not shot or injured or anything. . . . James, it must have been all a pretence—the whole thing. There can't be any other explanation."

All a pretence . . . !

Light suddenly dawned on Maguire. *Of course . . . !* Looking back now with his present knowledge, he could see how improbable the whole thing had been. The summary execution of a man for a wholly unproved offence. The burial group passing close to the house, when it could easily have kept away. . . . An elaborate pretence—and they must all have been in it. Connor and Donnelly and Regan, at that phoney tribunal. Boland shamming dead on the stretcher. Connor's men treating Maguire as a pariah afterwards. . . .

"Yes," he said, "you're right. It was a put-up job."

"But why?"

"I think the reason's fairly obvious—now. Connor must have decided I wasn't taking his threats seriously enough, after I'd been caught coming back from the cottage. To be safe, he had to convince me he was sufficiently ruthless to kill you if I gave the plot away—and he did it by pretending to execute Boland. Terror at one remove. . . . How stupid I was!"

"I don't see how you could have guessed."

"I ought to have done. I ought to have realised he wouldn't shoot one of his own men on so little evidence—and without a murmur from anyone else. But I wasn't feeling exactly clear-headed at the time—and it was all done so realistically. . . ."

He broke off, as a familiar voice sounded in the corridor. In a moment there was a knock on the door and Seamus O'Rourke came in, his hands outstretched in greeting. His face looked tired, but his step was brisk. His injured leg seemed miraculously better.

"James . . . ! Och, it's good to see you again. Safe, if not sound . . . !" He grinned at Nora, and pulled a chair up beside the bed. "How are you feeling?"

"Better every minute," Maguire said.

"That's good. They certainly gave you a beating, the young thugs. Not that it wasn't to be expected, if they had the chance—they must have felt quite sure at the time that it was you who'd given the plot away."

"Who did give it away, Seamus?"

O'Rourke shot a surprised glance at Nora.

"We hadn't got around to it," she told him. "There's been so much to talk about . . ."

"I suppose it was one of Connor's own men," Maguire said.

"Well, now," O'Rourke said, with a mischievous gleam, "if it's the official version you want, the Government had a security officer planted with the rebels from the start. . . . That's the story we put out to safeguard Nora and the children and that's the story we'll be sticking to for your own sake. Just to make sure there'll be no more beatings. . . . But if it's the truth about the informer you're after—well, who would it be but yourself?"

"It couldn't have been. . . ." Maguire began.

"Ah, but it was. It didn't happen the way you meant it to, James, but it happened all the same. . . ."

"How?"

"There was a picture of the Welcome Board in the *Dublin Examiner* yesterday morning—and by the grace of God I noticed it."

At once, everything became plain to Maguire. He remembered now—hadn't he seen the photographers at the site for the Press preview of the Pageant—and after the Board was erected . . . ? And he'd never given it a thought!

"So that was it."

"That's how it happened," O'Rourke said. "The Ogham script wasn't very clear in the picture, but it was clear enough for me to read my own name— and I wondered what the devil you'd been up to. I managed to decipher a bit more with the help of a magnifying glass and it didn't read like any welcome message to me—so I had myself driven down to the *Examiner* office and took a look at the original print. . . . If I hadn't known you so well, James, I'd have thought you'd gone clean out of your mind—but I did know you, and I remembered how Nora and the boys had gone away, and how worn out you'd seemed that day on the Hill. I hadn't a doubt it was all true. . . . So I thought up an excuse for not being at the Pageant, and rushed off to the Prime Minister—incidentally he wants to see you as soon as you're fit—and we set the wheels in motion. . . . I was tempted to say something when I rang you, something smart to let you know I'd read the message, but I didn't know how you were fixed or who'd be listening so it seemed safer not to. . . ."

Maguire gave a little nod.

"So there it is, James. ... You'll never be acclaimed a public hero, because the public will never know what happened, but it's thanks to you that a wicked enterprise came to nothing and that Connor got his deserts. If that man was a patriot, my name is Cromwell ... ! A little Caesar, that's what he was—and there are too damn many of them about these days. ... But, by God, he was clever. ..."

"He was a bit too clever," Maguire said, with a wry smile. He told O'Rourke about the Boland incident. "The ironical thing is that if Connor hadn't pretended to kill Boland his plot might have succeeded. He meant to terrorise me into silence—but what he actually did was to make me hate him and everything he stood for so much that I took a risk I probably wouldn't have considered otherwise. ... There's a lesson in that somewhere."

"There's another lesson I can think of," O'Rourke said, with a twinkle.

"What's that?"

"Always keep an eye on young fellows with trowels!" He pushed back his chair. "I think I'll go and see what they're up to and leave you two to finish your chat. See you later, Nora. And you, too, James. I hope that rib soon mends. ..." He turned at the door. "By the way, I hear the Pageant was a big success financially. A great day, James—in *every* way. A great day for Ireland!"

www.ingramcontent.com/pod-product-compliance
Ingram Content Group UK Ltd.
Pitfield, Milton Keynes, MK11 3LW, UK
UKHW040105010325
455690UK00002B/16